I0549712

Acknowledgments

In memory of Laurel Anne Clements, the first reader of this book.
January 10, 1978 – October 16, 2014
Rest in peace, sweet sister.

Thanks to Major Michael Grygar, U.S. Army, for his comments and suggestions. Thanks to Deborah Dillon for all of her assistance this past year—with the book and with everything else.

FINALIST
East Texas
Writers Guild
Book Awards
Mystery/Thriller
2016

FOR THE
CHILDREN'S
SAKE

N. M. Cedeño

Lucky Bat Books

A Lucky Bat Book

For the Children's Sake
Copyright 2015 by N. M. Cedeño
Cover Artist: Brandon Swann

Published by Lucky Bat Books
10 9 8 7 6 5 4 3 2

ISBN: 978-1-943588-01-5

Discover other titles by the author at nmcedeno.com

Your letter to the Reverend H. B. Gage is a document which, in my sight, if you had filled me with bread when I was starving, if you had sat up to nurse my father when he lay a-dying, would yet absolve me from the bonds of gratitude . . .

Common honour; not the honour of having done anything right, but the honour of not having done aught conspicuously foul; the honour of the inert: that was what remained to you. We are not all expected to be Damiens; a man may conceive his duty more narrowly, he may love his comforts better; and none will cast a stone at him for that . . .

Your Church and Damien's were in Hawaii upon a rivalry to do well: to help, to edify, to set divine examples. You having (in one huge instance) failed, and Damien succeeded, I marvel it should not have occurred to you that you were doomed to silence . . .

The world, in your despite, may perhaps owe you something, if your letter be the means of substituting once for all a credible likeness for a wax abstraction. For, if that world at all remember you, on the day when Damien of Molokai shall be named a Saint, it will be in virtue of one work: your letter to the Reverend H. B. Gage.

Extracted from Robert Louis Stevenson's open letter to C. M. Hyde, Feb. 25, 1890

CHAPTER 1

"The message says, 'Don't come. You can't help. I don't want you blamed if something happens to me.' That's the last I heard from him." Nate handed his phone to the detective, who took it in a gloved hand and dropped it in an evidence bag.

"You ignored the message and came anyway?" said the detective with a raised eyebrow.

"Not immediately, I got the message at eleven p.m. I was waiting to hear from him, but he didn't respond to any of my calls or texts. As time passed, I started to worry that something was seriously wrong. Then, at 1:26 a.m., I knew he was in trouble. I had to come."

"You left at one-thirty a.m. on a Monday morning and drove from San Marcos to Houston because of a feeling that your brother was in trouble."

"Yes," said Nate, hoping the detective believed him.

"Then, you found him dead on the ground outside his residence," said the detective, not hiding his skepticism.

"We've been over this. Ingall was dead when I found him. I pounded on the door until someone inside the building answered. I called 911. That's it."

The detective sighed. "No one else was around when you found your brother?"

"No one."

Detective Janwari stared at Nate, waiting for more information, maybe expecting Nate to tell him who had killed his brother.

An uncomfortable silence filled the space between them and chilled Nate, forcing him to speak again. "Look, I don't know what happened. I don't know why Ingall thought something might happen. He didn't tell me what was going on. Look at my phone. I tried to call, but he didn't answer. I sent messages, but he didn't respond. Check his phone. You'll see."

The detective stared, his face unmoving, disbelief in his dark, cold eyes. "Did your brother have any enemies?"

Nate stared back and gave a wry grimace, astounded that the detective had bothered asking that question. "Are you asking me if Father Ingall Bryan, voice of the Allergen Children's Rights Movement, had any enemies? Are you kidding me?"

A red flush filled the detective's face. "Did he have any personal enemies?"

"He didn't have time for anything personal. Ingall devoted all of his time to the children. He spent all his waking hours working for them. What you saw on television was Ingall's life. He was calm, patient, reasonable, and driven to fight for the sake of the children."

A sneer formed on Detective Janwari's lips, the gap between his upper front teeth making his mouth look like a lopsided jack-o'-lantern. "Those kids could wipe out eighty percent of the population with a touch, or simply by leaving skin oil on doors or, worse, in the water system. They're born killers."

"That's your opinion. That kind of reasoning fed the fear of HIV-infected people in the 1980s and led to the quarantining of people with leprosy for centuries. You might want to join the rest of us in the twenty-first century." Nate's retort dripped with contempt that he knew he should rein in, but the detective's response was the knee-jerk nonsense spewed by the mainstream media when they wanted to create paranoia and build suspense in order to gain the right number of eyeballs to sell premium advertisements.

Red-hot anger filled the detective's cheeks, and his hands clenched on the table. "Look, you bastard, I know what those kids can do. They killed my cousin."

Nate took a deep breath, but his anger bubbled up, and his words came faster and louder the more he spoke. "They killed both of my parents, too. Accidentally! No one could predict this mutation. No one went around trying to kill anyone. The kids' parents didn't know that their children's skin oils would cause other people to have allergic reactions. I'm not going to argue this with you. The courts have already decided that you can't charge an infant with murder, and you can't charge the parents with negligence or anything else. The problem was unforeseeable! If you want to find my brother's killer, look for people like you!"

The detective lunged forward across the interrogation table. Another officer standing to the side of the room leaped forward and grabbed Detective Janwari by the shoulders. Nate slid his chair back from the table, putting a few more inches between himself and the heaving, furious man. The second officer, a muscle-bound, dark-skinned man, shoved the shorter, leaner detective out of the interrogation room. Before the door slammed, Nate heard the detective say, "Whoever it was did the world a favor. I'd rather shake his hand than arrest him." Nate was left alone at the table to regain his composure.

Nate propped his elbows on the table and rubbed his eyes with the heels of his palms. It was past ten a.m., and he hadn't slept. He was exhausted, in need of a shower, and almost numb from the overwhelming wave of grief that threatened to eviscerate him. Ingall's absence left him mutilated in a way he never knew was possible. The ache was beyond anything he'd experienced in his thirty-five years of life. Even his parents' deaths hadn't hurt this badly. The image of Ingall lying on the ground, his eyes open, and small, bloody spots on his chest floated before his eyes.

An hour and a half later, as Nate was dozing at the table, Detective Janwari returned. "Mr. Bryan, you're free to go. Your cell phone GPS places you near your home in San Marcos until one-thirty a.m. Cell tower data and toll records show your car speeding through various checkpoints between two and three this morning. We know you weren't present at the time of the murder. However, you need to remain available for questioning."

The detective's rigidly controlled speech and mask of a face clearly indicated that he would rather arrest Nate than release him. Nate began to rise from his seat, but stopped as the detective spoke again.

"Your brother was trying to help evil people that barely qualify as human. If you ask me, he got what he deserved. Whoever killed him should be rewarded for protecting the rest of humanity. If you withhold information regarding this investigation, I will have you charged with interfering in the investigation, or even as an accessory to murder! All you crazies should be jailed for helping those monsters. I have two other active cases right now. Your brother's case will get all the attention I think it deserves! Public figure or not, he can wait his turn like everyone else!" The detective slammed Nate's phone down on the table in front of him.

"You aren't even going to look for his killer, are you?" said Nate as he glanced at his phone, surprised the screen hadn't cracked.

"I will investigate this case just like any other, because it's my job. I investigate the deaths of drug dealers and gang bangers, too. Don't you dare suggest I won't do what is required. I'll follow protocol with all due diligence. But I don't have to care for your brother's sorry ass any more than I'd care for a murdered serial killer.

Nate slid his phone into his pocket and refrained from responding, knowing the man was trying to provoke him into attacking, looking for a reason to jail him. He left the room and the police station as quickly as possible.

If the detective hated Ingall's work, and hated Nate for defending Ingall, Nate doubted that the detective would try very hard to find Ingall's killer. Many people had despised Ingall for championing the rights of children whom they saw as a threat to civilization. Nate realized that if he wanted justice, he would have to find out who had killed Ingall by himself. The knots left Nate's stomach. The bleak sense of emptiness evaporated, replaced by an ember of purpose. Nate was furious at the detective, enraged at the killer, and angry at the unfairness of having lost his brother so soon. He wanted to hit something, anything, more than he'd ever wanted to in his entire life. He'd fought to learn to control his temper, more or less taming himself as an adolescent. Controlled or not, the internal flame had never died out. His parents hadn't wrongly named him when they had called him Ignatius.

His parents had chosen the names Ingall and Ignatius for the twins before their birth. They had intended for the first born to be Ingall, which meant "messenger of God," and the second Ignatius, "meaning fiery," but they had changed their minds when Nate had come first, with a tuft of fiery red hair on his head and a demanding, irate cry. Ingall had been born less than a minute later, with brown hair and a calm, undemanding personality. Since Ignatius had been a mouthful, the name had quickly been shortened to Nate, which was far easier for his mother to yell and much less objectionable than Iggy.

Ingall had certainly been the messenger, even when people had not wanted to hear the message. He'd earned more than his share of enemies. One of them had killed him. Nate burned to find that person.

It was only noon. He had plenty of time to begin asking questions, and he knew where to start: Ingall's office.

As he drove, some of the roaring fire in Nate's gut dissipated to a more controlled level. He pictured it as being like a Bunsen burner that he could adjust at will, a mental trick he'd used for years. He began to wonder what Ingall would say to him about this situation.

Parking his car in front of Ingall's office building off the Katy Freeway in Houston, Nate sat and wondered whether he was making the right decision. Biochemistry professors don't investigate murders. They leave that to the police. However, if he were to walk away and leave the case to a detective who felt that Ingall had gotten what he'd deserved, regret would consume Nate for the rest of his life. Still, Nate was conflicted. Ingall had specifically told him not to come, and Nate usually hated himself when he didn't take Ingall's advice. The lack of sleep, lack of food, and shock of Ingall's death had him on a roller coaster of emotion. He seemed to be experiencing all the stages of grief in turn every half hour. He tried to think dispassionately about his course of action, but found he couldn't do it. He needed sleep but didn't want to rest until he was exhausted enough to fall quickly and deeply asleep. If he were to try sleeping now, being as wound up as he was, he'd never manage it. His brain was in too much turmoil.

Nate fell back to thinking about the events that had led up to his discovery of Ingall's body. At least he hadn't told the detective why Ingall might have expected Nate to come, even without a phone call.

Once, when Ingall had broken his leg, Nate had had an overwhelming desire to call him immediately. Another time, when Nate had been struggling with the decision to quit working in pharmaceutical development and return to academia, Ingall had called to ask what was bothering him. Neither had ever known the specifics of the other's problem before he called. He just knew that he had to reach out and call. Ingall had known he might be in danger. He had known Nate would call, and, failing to get an answer, Nate had come. Ingall had known that, if were to die, Nate might be the first to find him. Logically, the person with the body is the first investigated. Well, he'd crossed that bridge already. It was too late to take Ingall's advice not to drive to Houston. Finally, Nate reasoned that Ingall had never said that he couldn't investigate, and the fire in his stomach demanded that he investigate. So Nate flung his car door open and got out to start his investigation.

Nate stepped out into Houston's near-perpetual midday humidity. Like New Orleans, Houston had been built on swampy land laced with bayous. Flooding was common after the heavy rains brought by tropical weather systems. Clouds covered the sky, making the air even heavier and the day even grayer, which seemed fitting for Nate's first day without his brother.

Deacon Matthias Boudreaz greeted Nate at the door of the building, his eyes red and glassy, his lips pressed together in a sad line. He grabbed Nate's hand in both of his and shook it, words of sympathy tumbling out of his mouth. "I can't believe he's dead. I can't, I can't—I am so sorry for your loss, Nate."

"It's your loss, too," Nate said.

"We've lost a brother," he said, his eyes watering again. "Can you tell me what you know? What happened? Do the police have any suspects? How did you find him?"

"He'd sent me a text, and I was worried he might be in some kind of trouble. I called and texted him back. He didn't respond. I waited for hours, hoping he'd contact me, but he didn't. Finally, I knew something was wrong, so I drove down here. I got to the residence at 3:45 a.m.; you know the place, right?"

"The new diocesan residence for nonparochial priests? Yes, I've been there."

"I found Ingall lying on the grass next to the parking area. He'd been shot twice in the chest. He was dead when I got to him."

The image of Ingall's dead body flashed before Nate's eyes. It felt unreal, like something out of a movie. Nate wanted to deny what he'd seen. He wanted to tell the deacon that it had to be some kind of mistake, that Ingall couldn't be dead, but he knew he couldn't. He felt hollow, like a walking empty shell.

"No one saw anything or heard the shots?" the deacon pressed.

"No, that side of the residence, overlooking the parking area, contains the kitchen and breakfast area downstairs, and the upper floors have work spaces, offices, and an exercise room. The bedrooms are on the other side. One of the priests told me that since the building is so close to the freeway, it was built with soundproofing. Everyone was asleep. I had to bang on the door for a minute or two before anyone came out. Old Father Martinez went and sat with him until the police arrived."

"Father Martinez? He retired last year after he had a stroke, didn't he?" asked Matthias.

"I don't know. This Father Martinez looked to be about a hundred years old, and he walked with a cane and a bad limp."

"That's the priest I mean," said Matthias.

Nate remembered the gray-skinned, gaunt priest praying over Ingall. To Nate's relief, Father Martinez had closed Ingall's eyes. The cold blankness that remained, where once bright and spirited blue eyes had been, chilled Nate. At least Ingall hadn't been lying in an obvious pool of blood. Beneath the lamppost that illuminated the parking area, no blood had been visible, except the two dark spots on his chest. Nate wondered whether the blood had spread down into the thick layer of St. Augustine grass beneath him. Shaking visions of Ingall's dead body from his mind, Nate refocused on why he'd come to see Matthias. "Have the police been here to collect Ingall's laptop and papers?"

"Yes. They came around eight this morning." Here, at last, a smile wavered on Matthias's face. "You should have seen the look on the crime-scene processor's face when he saw Father Ingall's office. The poor man looked horrified."

Nate's eyes lit with humor, momentarily lifting the dark cloud around him. Ingall had been a genius, a holy person, maybe even a saint, but he had been a disaster when it came to paperwork. His whole office was covered in mountains of paper: old lists, books, studies, documents of all sorts. Only Ingall could discern the system behind his stacks. Ingall could pick a document from a pile without pause when he had needed something. He had liked to hold things in his hand and flip through the pages. He'd had electronic reading devices, but invariably printed out all kinds of things. He would go through reams of paper faster than everyone else in the office combined. "Did they try to take it all with them for analysis?" asked Nate.

"No, a man looked through the piles, but realized most of it was irrelevant to the case. They took his computer and a copy of his schedule. The officer seemed most interested in the threats he'd received lately."

Nate nodded, but wondered whether Detective Janwari would thoroughly investigate the threats, since he obviously sympathized with them. Most of the people who had threatened Ingall had lost family members to the touch of Allergen Children. The threats had never frightened Ingall. He could see the grief behind the words and had written letters of condolence to each person, offering comfort and prayers. Most of the writers had either forgotten or had never known that the twins' parents had died from inadvertent contact with such a child. Ingall would tell the angry ones about his parents' deaths and explain his reasons for fighting for the children. Sometimes, that was the end of it. Other times, people replied with donations for the research to cure the children.

"How was the research progressing?" Nate asked. "The last time we spoke, Ingall said one researcher working on the problem had made a breakthrough that looked like it might resolve the children's situation."

Ingall's focus in life had been to solve the biggest social conundrum of the generation. In the past twenty years, massive amounts of research had been done to try to explain the children's condition. Most had been born in or near petrochemical hubs like Houston and had grandparents who worked in the petrochemical industry and suffered from severe seasonal allergies. The grandparents had been given a particular allergy medicine in the ten to fifteen years before the births of their own children. Research had found that the Allergen Children's parents were carriers of single copies of a new genetic mutation. When a child carrying a double copy of the newly identified genetic mutation was several weeks old, the toxin in the child's skin oils became strong enough to cause serious allergic reactions in other people. By six months, the child's touch was deadly to noncarriers of the mutation.

The first incident to draw national attention involved an infant being placed in a day care. Two caregivers died of anaphylactic shock and an emergency medical technician responding to the call almost died. Scientists eventually identified the cause of the anaphylaxis to be a chemical in the infant's skin oils. The infant's parents found themselves besieged on all sides, their child quarantined as a biohazard.

More deaths occurred as more cases emerged. The children with the double mutation were placed into quarantined facilities while medical researchers tried to devise a cure. Then, the unthinkable happened. A six-month-old child who hadn't been identified as a double mutation carrier went on vacation at a water theme park in the arms of his unknowing parents. More than a thousand people died when the toxin from the child's skin got into the water. Making matters worse, the child and his parents vanished. Police found evidence that they had fled the country under false identities. No further trace of them was ever found. People lived in fear of a repeat incident or a larger, targeted attack on a city's water supply. In response, all hell broke loose in cities where the Allergen Children were housed. Police in riot gear had to stop angry mobs from torching quarantine camps in Louisiana and Philadelphia.

Into the fray had stepped Ingall, calling for calm, for healing, for new research, and for the rights of the children. He had become the voice of reason and the target of enmity, taking all manner of insults for his work. He had been spat upon, physically attacked, and verbally mocked, but he had kept working. In the last three years, he had tried to turn the tide of public opinion, speaking at churches, city halls, and congressional hearings.

"Father Ingall was excited about the research results," Matthias responded in answer to Nate's question. "He thought that the final push for the detainees' release was approaching. He had a meeting with Dr. Willett King two days ago, on Saturday, and with some of the older children in Camp Lambda yesterday. We were supposed to have lunch today so that we could sit down and discuss the new developments and set his schedule. He said that the path was finally clear."

Nate hesitated as they walked down the hall toward Ingall's office and looked at Deacon Matthias. "He said those words? 'The path is finally clear?'"

"Yes. Why?"

He shook his head and didn't answer. Whenever Ingall had talked of paths, it had meant choices in life that he'd had to make. He wouldn't have used the phrase to refer to a plan to release the detainees. Deacon Matthias had only been with Ingall for a year. He didn't recognize the significance of the phrase, but Nate did.

Nate filed the comment away for future consideration and focused on his upcoming task. Matthias unlocked Ingall's office door. They stood in the doorway and surveyed the disaster. The only empty space in the room was where the police had removed Ingall's laptop from his desk. The rest of the room was as Ingall had left it: complete chaos.

"Do you know where his lists are?" Nate asked.

"The smallest pile on the desk," said Matthias, pointing to a stack of torn pieces of scrap paper, sticky notes, magnetic-backed "Things to Do" notepads, pages torn from planning notebooks, and paper napkins, all with numbered lists on them.

Ingall had been a list maker. From the mundane to the vital, he had only remembered to do something if he'd written it on a list, which was why Deacon Matthias had been assigned to keep him on schedule. What Ingall had rated as a priority had gone on his list, and those items hadn't always been what others had agreed were important. Most of the time, Ingall had made one list a day, not bothering to write the date on the list. Consequently, determining the age of a list could be difficult. Sometimes, he'd plan a whole week on one sheet of paper, drawing arrows and moving things around from day to day as needed. Nate picked up the stack of papers and handed it to Matthias. "Any chance you could find the most recent lists?"

"I'll try," Matthias said, and began to shuffle the lists through his hands. He read a few of the lists, shifted them to the bottom of the pile and kept going. After a minute, he paused and handed Nate a piece of paper. It read:

1. *Toothpaste*
2. *Meet Mons. Gilla'a for lunch*
3. *Dr. King new info 4pm*
4. *Take supplies to camp*

Announce Park's Solution???

Each item was listed, one beneath the other, down a quarter of a sheet of printer paper. The phrase "Announce Park's Solution???" had been written at an angle across the bottom, as if it hadn't been part of the original list. The words were hurriedly scrawled and circled four times, unlike the neatly printed and numbered items of the list.

"How old is this one?" Nate asked.

"He had lunch with Monseigneur Gilla'a Saturday. Father Ingall did see Dr. Willett King that day, too. The supplies were for the older children at Camp Lambda. As I mentioned, Father Ingall was there yesterday."

"So this is from the day before yesterday, Saturday?"

"Probably. He had intended to get to the camps Saturday, but the meeting with Dr. King ran longer than expected," said Matthias.

"What does 'Announce Park's solution' mean?"

Matthias hesitated, looking uncomfortable. "Dr. Park is one of the researchers. Father Ingall said that Dr. Park was 'thinking outside the box' and approaching things differently than Dr. King. She'd found a resolution for the problem, but it's not a cure. I could tell you how it works, but Father Ingall didn't want it discussed until it was announced. He was afraid it would be warped by rumors. Undoing misinformation takes herculean efforts, since the incorrect version gets perpetuated on the Internet. Consider the damage that was caused by the reports linking vaccines to autism long after any possible link was debunked." Matthias smiled apologetically.

"I understand. I'll go talk to the doctors and get the information straight from them, if you'd rather not repeat it. Keep looking at the pile and see if there's a list for yesterday. He sent me a message that suggested that he thought he might have trouble. Anything he wrote down for yesterday might give us an idea of what he had on his mind."

Deacon Matthias reviewed the rest of the scraps of paper for several more minutes, muttering to Nate as he worked. "This is last month. Two weeks ago. Lunch with the bishop was on a Friday, not last week but the week before. He met with Senator Kingsley four days ago to argue against legislation requiring sterilization of the children in the camps. This list with the meeting with the Tolokonskys could be last Monday, but he met with them several times a month, so it's hard to say."

Finally, having gone through the pile at least twice, he looked up and shook his head at Nate. "I don't see a list for yesterday, but he didn't work on Sundays at the office. He frequently gave guest sermons at different churches in the diocese. Yesterday, he also visited the children's camp and attended a fundraiser at St. John Vianney Church."

"You kept his schedule straight and resolved conflicting appointments for him. Did the police take your copy of his schedule?" asked Nate, trying to decide whether it was worth it to try to sit down in Ingall's flood of paper.

"I gave them a copy of his online calendar, but I still have access to it." Matthias returned the stack of notes to its spot on Ingall's desk.

"Would you make me a copy, too? If we can't find notes saying what Ingall had on his mind, I may have to talk to all the people he saw recently. He didn't have anything scheduled for late last night, did he?" asked Nate, as he moved away from an unbalanced pile of papers that threatened to cascade down on him.

"Come to my office, and I'll get you a copy of his calendar. I didn't have anything on his schedule for last night, but you know how he was."

Matthias and Nate left Ingall's office and walked down the hall to Matthias's sparser, smaller office.

Matthias sat at his desk and reviewed Ingall's calendar. "As I was saying, he didn't have anything scheduled for late last night. At least, not officially. If someone called and asked to come see him, he'd say yes, no matter the hour. He was always doing things like that. I've seen him argue for the children in city council meetings well past midnight, attend a prayer breakfast at seven the next morning, then spend the rest of the day teaching and counseling children in the camps. Some days he forgot to eat." Tears reappeared in the deacon's eyes as he spoke.

"I appreciate what you did to keep him going." Ingall had always been thin. He had worked hard and eaten little. He'd never been unhealthy, just tall and gangly. Like the actor Jimmy Stewart in classic movies from the 1930s, his weight had never quite filled out his tall frame. Nate lightly grasped Deacon Matthias's shoulder in an effort to comfort the man. His own eyes burned.

Both men stared in silence at the computer screen, momentarily lost in thought.

Finally, Nate blinked rapidly to dispel the sensation in his eyes and forced himself to focus on the matter at hand. "Could you tell me about the threats Ingall had received? Anything you felt was more serious in nature?" Nate settled into an uncomfortable, flat-bottomed visitor's chair across the desk from Matthias.

Deacon Matthias looked at Nate with searching hazel eyes. "Are you sure you should be investigating this? Why not leave it to the police? He was a prominent public figure. They'll want this solved quickly."

"I want it solved quickly, too. However, I want it done right. Detective Janwari, who is in charge of the case, has no sympathy for the children and no appreciation for Ingall's work. I don't trust him to want Ingall's murder solved." Anger filled Nate's voice as he spoke and his hands balled into fists on his knees.

Matthias considered Nate's answer with a troubled and skeptical expression before he said, "We only had one person threaten Ingall repeatedly whom I felt could be dangerous. You've probably seen him on the news—Landon Piccone. Father Ingall tried to speak to him but couldn't get past the man's grief and anger at losing his children. His toddler son and infant daughter died sixteen years ago in a day-care center when an Allergen Child was placed there. His babies went into anaphylactic shock and died after the caregiver picked each child up in turn to place them in cribs for a nap. The caregiver turned out to be immune, but most of the other children in the center died that day. Mr. Piccone hates that Father Ingall wanted to help free the very child who killed his kids. He blames the child's parents, too. Since the parents are our biggest donors and frequently speak out for the rights of the children, Mr. Piccone refused to speak to Father Ingall."

"Who are the parents?"

"The Tolokonskys."

Nate nodded comprehension. Ivan Tolokonsky was the wealthiest and most vocal family advocate for the rights of the isolated children. He'd inherited his father's five-man petrochemical company and had made himself a billionaire by inventing a more environmentally sound method for extracting oil from shale to replace the questionable practice of hydraulic fracturing, or "fracking." He and his wife were carriers of the mutation, as was one of their daughters. Their other daughter and son had inherited the dangerous double mutation and had been in medical quarantine camps for most of their lives. Now that the kids were teenagers, their parents were advocating for their return to society, demanding an end to their enforced isolation. The Tolokonskys had created body suits to cover all exposed skin below the neck to keep the teens from spreading the dangerous exudate. They felt that, with appropriate caution, the teens could be released to live normal lives. The Tolokonskys spent millions of dollars supporting research for a cure and lobbying for the children's rights.

Deacon Matthias said, "Mr. Piccone tried to have criminal charges filed against the Tolokonskys' son."

"For what?"

"Murder," said Matthias.

"Murder? He must have known that wouldn't work."

"That didn't stop Mr. Piccone from trying. After that, he filed a civil suit against the Tolokonskys. He didn't win, but the lawyers probably made a hefty fee out of the situation. When that failed, he picketed outside the Tolokonskys' house and offices until the Tolokonskys were forced to get a restraining order against him. Before the Tolokonskys' youngest daughter was born, Piccone filed a complaint with the police that the birth would be a threat to public safety and requested that the baby be quarantined from the moment of birth. The Tolokonskys had to fight to keep the girl until the test results came back showing that she only had one copy of the mutation."

"Has Piccone threatened violence?" asked Nate.

"He claims his main concern is public safety, but yes, he did threaten Father Ingall. He was afraid that by going into the camps, Father Ingall might inadvertently spread the exudate from the children and endanger more lives. He said Father Ingall had to stop visiting the camps, or he would find a way to make him stop."

Nate considered the statement and tried to match it with what he knew of the man who'd made it. "That's a vague threat. Given his record for legal action, maybe Piccone was going to try a method of legal recourse."

"Oh, he did that, too. Mr. Piccone tried to get a judge to order Father Ingall to wear a full biohazard suit when inside the camps. Father Ingall refused. He said he wasn't afraid of the children harming him. Also, he didn't want to compromise his standing with the children. They trusted him. To suddenly wear a biohazard suit around them would make it look like he didn't trust them."

"What kind of protective gear did he wear? He must have taken precautions of some sort. He wasn't immune to the toxin." Ingall might have ventured where few others dared, but he had not been stupid. He'd have been careful doing it.

"He wore his black pants, a black shirt with the collar, and a black suit coat, looking very formal and traditional. You know how little he cared about clothes. He wore variations of the same outfit every day. When he saw the littlest children, Father Ingall would wear a wetsuit under his clothes. The little ones are more dangerous because of drool, sneezing, and the various bodily fluids they can't control. Babies and toddlers are quite messy. For the older kids, he would put on black disposable gloves, but that's all. The personnel in the camps who aren't immune and have direct contact with the children wear specially made long-sleeved scrubs and gloves. Everyone has to follow safety procedures before leaving the camp. Like the camp personnel, Father Ingall would shower and change clothes, including his shoes, before leaving the camp. The camp laundry would sanitize everything for him, so he would have an outfit ready and waiting for him before his next visit. The families of the children do the same except, since they are mostly immune, they typically don't need to wear gloves or protective clothing."

"Have they figured out the inheritance pattern?" Nate's biochemist curiosity was kicking in. He'd talked to Ingall about the children before, but Ingall had never pushed him to join in the research. He'd probably known that if he were to push, Nate might have retreated from the matter altogether. A wave of guilt washed through Nate. He could have spent more time with Ingall if he'd joined the research. Now, it was too late. He tried to listen to Matthias, his curiosity stamped out by guilt.

"Each parent carries one copy of the mutation, so each child has a chance to get either a good copy or a bad copy of the gene from each parent. That makes a one in four chance of a sibling getting two good copies of the gene and not even being a carrier."

"Was anything else bothering Ingall? Any other problems with people? Anything at all?"

Matthias hesitated, winding his hands nervously around each other. "He had a personal issue crop up, but I can't imagine that was related to his death. It didn't bother Father Ingall."

Matthias's hesitation and apparent discomfort spoke volumes. "Personal issue" had been Ingall's shorthand way of saying an employee or volunteer had fallen in love with him. Ingall had never been bothered by that sort of thing, since it had happened often enough. However, that didn't mean the person involved wasn't disturbed, embarrassed, unhappy, pining, or unbalanced. Ingall had not had the time nor the interest for intimate, personal relationships. His work had absorbed him so completely that he had rarely thought about physical attraction until bluntly faced with the results of it. Then, he would fall back on his training from his former career as a psychologist, before turning to the priesthood, and gently rebuff his admirer.

"Okay," Nate said, suddenly wanting to laugh, "if you don't think that's related, I won't ask for the details yet, but if I run into a roadblock, I'll be back asking for more information." Nate realized he was very emotionally unstable. He didn't know whether he would laugh or cry at any given moment.

Matthias nodded, visibly relieved that Nate wasn't going to make him talk about it. Whoever the person was, Matthias didn't want to drag any names through the mud. Besides, such matters were best handled with discretion. The fewer the people who knew, the fewer the wagging tongues. Gossip could spread like a wildfire. Matthias transferred a copy of Ingall's schedule to Nate's phone.

The conversation swung to the matter of funeral planning, a process that took almost an hour. The entire experience was bizarre for Nate, as if moving through a dream. Choosing readings and songs for the funeral mass was traumatic, and discussing obituary details made him want to rebel against the whole process. Ingall's death felt obscenely unfair.

The more he thought about the injustice of Ingall's murder, the more Nate wanted to find the person responsible. Though it was obvious that the police didn't care, Nate did, and maybe that was enough. He may not have the contacts to do background checks, but he had internet access. He could ask questions and look for answers as well as anybody.

With the details of the funeral somewhat hammered out, Nate took his leave at three o'clock, finally ready to give in to sleep. He shook the deacon's hand and saw himself out.

As Nate climbed into his car, his phone rang. A glance showed a name he hadn't seen in more than six months.

Chapter 2

"Hello?" said Nate cautiously, unsure what to expect.

"Nate? Hi. I'm so, so very sorry to hear about Ingall," said Loriana's gravelly, deep voice, which was midway between Lauren Bacall in *The Big Sleep* and Jodie Foster in *Silence of the Lambs*.

"How did you hear?" Nate asked.

"I read it online," she said.

Loriana Montilla had been the love of Nate's life. He had loved her more than anyone, so, conversely, he could hate her more than anyone. Their disagreements, while never physical, had become more and more volatile before he'd finally called off their engagement. He had realized a month before the wedding that they were fundamentally incompatible. Nate believed in God, in an individual's ability to make a difference in the world, and in the value of altruism. Most of all, he had believed in Ingall and in the importance of his work. Loriana was cynical, self-contained, agnostic, and doubtful that Ingall would be able to accomplish anything. She had believed that donating to Ingall's work was a waste of financial resources. At the same time, Loriana was self-motivated, level-headed, intelligent, unfailingly polite to everyone, goal-oriented, and competent at most everything she tried. She didn't expect anyone to help her reach her goals, so she worked hard, putting her best effort into everything she did. She had always said that failure or success was within her own control. Nate had not been able to make her see that life wasn't that simple for everyone.

"Do you know what happened?" she asked.

"Not yet," he said.

"The article said that you reported his death and that the police took you into custody."

"I did, and they did. They figured out that I didn't know anything and couldn't have done it. So they let me go."

"What were you doing at Ingall's place in the middle of the night?"

"If I told you, you wouldn't believe me," he said with a snap of anger in his voice. He heard her sharp intake of breath at the harshness of his answer. His jaw clenched. The memory of how little faith she had had in anything she couldn't see or measure set his nerves on edge. She wouldn't have openly mocked his assertion that he had gone because he had known Ingall was dead, but she wouldn't have been able to mask her skepticism either. He could still see the look of disbelief she had put on when she had disagreed with him, her slightly crooked nose wrinkled and her full, dark eyebrows drawn together almost in a single mass across her forehead.

"I wanted to say I'm sorry for your loss, and that I understand the importance of Ingall's work. Goodbye, Nate." The call terminated.

Nate tossed the phone down onto the seat next to him, impatient with his display of temper. She'd called out of concern for him. She didn't deserve his brusque response. Nate had fought to learn to control his fiery temper as a teenager. He'd succeeded so well; few of his colleagues knew he had a temper. Yet Loriana could unleash it with a word.

He ran his hands through his thinning red hair and over the stubble on his face. His energy levels were ebbing, his eyes trying to close as he drove. Nate drove to a Holiday Inn

Express, checked in, crawled into bed, and slept for two hours. After a snack, a shower, and a shave, he was ready to work.

Scanning the information from Matthias, he thought the Tolokonskys seemed to be the best place to start. They had been working toward the same goals as Ingall, had met with him frequently, and had supported his work financially. Either Ivan Tolokonsky or his wife, Vera, might know what had been on Ingall's mind, what had worried him, what had excited him, and maybe what "Park's Solution" entailed.

Dr. King might also have some answers, since he'd seen Ingall the day before he died.

Nate decided to contact both the doctor and the Tolokonskys and ask to see them. Hopefully, they would be willing to talk to him. Ingall had been a people person, solid and discreet, with an ear meant for confidences and a mind made for advising the troubled. On the other hand, Nate's methods of persuasion involved arguing logically and proving a point to a reasonable certainty, within a measure that included a standard deviation for error. In Nate's experience, most people didn't use those methods in everyday life. He didn't even consider himself to be socially adept.

Nate left messages for the Tolokonskys and Dr. Willett King, then went to the nearest restaurant serving Tex-Mex. It was after five o'clock, and he hadn't eaten a full meal since yesterday. He ordered beef fajitas, flour tortillas, guacamole, and a Dos Equis and ate, alone with his thoughts of Ingall. At least their parents had died first, or he would have had to inform them of Ingall's death. As it was, only an uncle, an aunt, and two cousins remained to be notified, and they had dropped contact with the family when Ingall had begun his work on behalf of the children. Nate didn't care whether they heard of Ingall's death through news articles or not.

Nate remembered his parents' deaths. They'd died in a tragic incident involving an Allergen Child at a grocery store. His father had randomly selected a cart from the lines of carts by the entrance of the store and then turned it over to their mother. He had collapsed with breathing difficulties a moment later, just moments after entering the store. Nate's mother had then reached down to help, and immediately began to gasp for breath herself. A teenage clerk had run for doses of epinephrine, standard in most public places since the advent of the Allergen Children. The doses had been on the opposite side of the building, and the clerk had fumbled while administering them, lacking the self-confidence and experience to use the shots quickly. By the time the clerk had injected the medicine, it was too late. The whole incident had played out on the store's security monitor in front of the doors. News agencies had demanded copies of the video and had replayed the deaths on the nightly news for three days until something more sensational had come along.

The subsequent police investigation had found secretions from an Allergen Child, one that had probably been less than a year old, based on the size of the handprints on the handle of the cart. In spite of police efforts to find them, the family of the child had never been identified. No one had come forward with information. All in all, Nate couldn't blame them. The family would have seen the child grow up in a quarantine camp if they had come forward. The parents had probably decided to keep the child at home for as long as they could, hoping for a cure. Six months later, Ingall had decided to devote himself to helping the Allergen Children. He'd said he had felt "called" to work for them. Ingall's bishop had agreed and reassigned him. In no time at all, Ingall had become the public face of those fighting to help the children.

As he lingered over a large basket of salted tortilla chips, Nate's mind meandered back to Loriana. The last thing she'd said was that she understood the importance of Ingall's work. Nate wondered why she had said that. She'd openly disparaged everything Ingall had done when they had been dating. None of Nate's arguments had had the smallest effect on her opinion. Something cataclysmic must have happened for her to have changed her mind. Maybe her sister had given birth to an Allergen Child. Nate doubted anything short of personal experience with the tragedy could have opened her to seeing things differently. He was considering whether to call her back when his phone rang.

"Hello?" he said, expecting Loriana's gravelly voice.

"Mr. Bryan? This is Dr. Willett King. You left a message for me to call you back?"

"Hello, Doctor. Thanks for calling me back." Nate gathered his scattered thoughts. "I'm Father Ingall Bryan's brother. You probably heard that he . . . died, um . . . was murdered." Nate paused to stabilize his voice, which had started to crack. "Would you be willing to tell me about the work you are doing and how my brother was involved in it?" Nate forced himself to bury the memories of Ingall's fallen body and sightless eyes that had sprung instantly into his mind with the mention of his name. If all he did was envision his dead brother, he wouldn't find the truth or identify the killer. Instead, he pictured Ingall cheering him to success, as Ingall often had done when they had been teens playing sports.

"The police already contacted me about his death. Please accept my condolences on your loss. Are you interested in carrying on his work, Mr. Bryan?"

"Thank you. I'm interested in seeing his work continue, but, right now, I'm trying to find out what was going on in his life before he died."

"I see." The doctor hesitated. "Shouldn't you leave the investigation to the police?"

"The detective in charge is not sympathetic to the children. I don't trust him to want to find Ingall's killer."

"Are you looking for revenge? Because if that's the case, I have no interest in meeting you."

"No. Ingall wouldn't want that. I only want to know the truth about what happened. I want to know what was going on in Ingall's life, and I don't anticipate that the police will be willing to keep me apprised of the investigation." Nate kept his voice low, to avoid being overheard by others in the restaurant.

Silence met him from the other end of the line. Nate was about to inquire whether the doctor was still on the line when the man spoke. "Can you come see me this evening at seven p.m.? I have a late meeting, but I should be free by then."

"That would be fine. Thank you, Dr. King. Where would you like to meet?"

"At my offices in Memorial Hermann Research Center Hospital off Gessner Road. The receptionist at the information desk in the lobby can direct you to me. I'll leave your name at the desk, so that whoever is there knows you are expected. We've had some problems with protesters trying to get into my offices lately. Only people I put on the list are allowed to come up to see me."

"I understand. See you at seven."

As he put the phone back in his pocket, it began to ring again.

"Mr. Bryan? This is Ivan Tolokonsky. Your brother's death is a great tragedy for all of us who are working to help the children. We grieve his loss with you."

Given the doctor's hesitant response to his inquiries, Nate decided to take a different tack with Tolokonsky, and showed more interest in his cause. "Thank you. Could we meet to discuss my brother's work? I want to know how things stand now that he is gone. I'm sure the police will be contacting you, if they haven't already done so, but I wanted to hear firsthand if you knew of anyone threatening my brother or trying to block the work you were doing together."

"I would be happy to discuss your brother's work with you. Father Ingall was a blessing for my family. He was of great help to my son and daughter in the camp, acting as their teacher, therapist, and advisor. We will miss his counsel. He knew how to quell the hotheaded ideas and rebellion of the teenagers and keep them working for a positive outcome in the future. He kept their hopes alive. Moving forward without him will be a challenge."

"When and where could we meet?"

"I am on a tight schedule today, but tomorrow morning is free. Can you come to my house at nine a.m.?"

"Yes, I can," said Nate.

Mr. Tolokonsky agreed to text Nate his address, and ended the conversation. Nate left the restaurant with a little time to kill before the meeting with Dr. King. Back in his hotel room, he left a message for Detective Janwari to let him know where he was staying, and then he sat down to research current events relating to the Allergen Children and Ingall.

Nate was familiar with the background of the problem and the swaying public sentiments on how to handle the matter. The thing that prodded him to research was the word "rebellion" that Mr. Tolokonsky had used. Nate had always considered the Allergen Children to be small children, although common sense told him that many of them were teenagers. The years had passed, and he, like a relative who seldom sees a young family member, was shocked to learn how much the children had grown. The oldest of the children in

Houston camps could easily be nineteen by now. They weren't children anymore, but young adults. Some people at that age rarely thought about the long-term consequences of their behavior. They tended to be rash, impulsive, and hormonal. Given their situation, they were probably angry as well. No wonder talk of sterilization was picking up in the news. These kids were on the cusp of adulthood. If they were aware of the ideas being bandied about in the press regarding their futures, they might be preparing for all-out war.

The sites Nate found gave him little comfort. Dozens of articles recommended that the children be sterilized and imprisoned for life, several recommended that they be "put down," and one particularly radical site called for burning the camps in hopes that the cleansing fires would obliterate their very essence from the earth. Then, Nate reviewed the pages calling for the children's rights and advocating for their release from the camps. The tone of the comments on each of the sites ranged from reasonable to impassioned to violent, with the most recent comments being the most violent. Trouble was brewing on both sides of the issue. Ingall had probably seen the trouble on the horizon.

After digesting as much of the information as he could, Nate closed up the research and went to meet Dr. King.

∽

Monday evening, Camp Lambda.

"FATHER INGALL IS dead," said Omar. "He was murdered, probably to stop him from helping us. We need to be ready. We could have a mob attack here like they did in Pennsylvania and Louisiana." His somber, black eyes surveyed the room to make sure everyone was listening.

"So let them come! One touch and they're dead!" said thir-teen-year-old Jeremy.

"Do you really think they'd let you touch them? A mob could set fire to this place from the outside and burn us all to death. They could lob in grenades or destroy the building with a bomb!" said Sam, his ebony skin taut across his broad cheeks and flattened nose.

"That's why our dad had the panic room built," said Sandr, trying to quell any sense of panic that might rise from Sam's more blunt pronouncement.

"And why we have emergency drills once a month," said his sister, Anya, in a quieter voice. Her crossed arms hugged her slender, tense body.

"I know, but we need to keep our eyes open here. Things are escalating. What we really need is a way to get more of the public on our side," said Omar. He ran a hand through his thick black hair. A tall young man with Mediterranean looks and olive skin, Omar was the oldest detainee.

"Then we need to make our voices heard. We need to get the public to see us as people before it's too late," said Anya.

"What about Father Ingall's funeral?" Sam asked. "Do you think that would be the place to show the world that we can be trusted in public?"

"Yeah!" said Sandr. "They should let us go to the funeral. We could wear the suits Dad designed. We could talk to reporters. People would see that we aren't violent killing machines plotting to wipe out humanity. Dad could arrange it!"

Omar frowned in thought as everyone awaited his response. At nineteen, thanks to his intelligence and force of character, he was the acknowledged leader of the group. He'd completed a degree in political science and another in engineering from an online program at the University of

Texas. He nodded decisively. "We should go to the funeral. Father Ingall was our counselor and teacher. We should have the right to go and mourn him. We'll talk to reporters, but I don't want the funeral to be a circus. We'll only talk to them after it's over. Sandr, can you talk to your father about the protective suits? Can you ask him to bring four?"

"Only four?" Anya asked.

"Only the oldest should go. The younger ones are still too hotheaded to control themselves in public," he said with a suppressive frown at Jeremy. "We need to make a good impression. Only Sam, Anya, Sandr, and I should go."

A groan of protest escaped the younger members of the group, about a dozen young teens ranging in age from thirteen to fifteen, all gathered in the lounge area. No one verbalized disagreement with Omar's decision, although a few of the teens gave him looks laden with discontent or disappointment. Of the four Omar had selected to go, Sam, at eighteen, was the next oldest, and Anya, at fifteen and a half, was the youngest. Her brother, Sandr, was seventeen. Their father had designed the protective clothing that they hoped to wear under their own clothes to protect the rest of the world from them.

At that moment, Elizaveta, the younger sister of Sandr and Anya, hurried into the room, followed by her parents, signaling the start of evening visiting hours. As a carrier of only a single copy of the mutation, fourteen-year-old Elizaveta didn't secrete the deadly chemical from her skin, and was allowed to live outside the camp. Blonde and blue-eyed like the rest of her family, she'd also inherited her father's drive and obstinate streak. She carried a plastic-wrapped plate of cookies.

"I see we've interrupted a meeting," said Ivan Tolokonsky as he put his arm around his daughter Anya and kissed her cheek. "What are y'all plotting now?" he asked the group at large.

"Well, Sir, we want to go to Father Ingall's funeral," said Omar.

Ivan's eyes jerked away from his children and studied Omar's serious face. "I see."

"We thought that might be the best place to show the world that we are humans, not animals or killers who have to be locked up for life," said Sam.

"Can you get us the suits you made, Dad?" asked Sandr.

Ivan Tolokonsky looked at the crowd of children in the lounge area around him. "How many?"

"Only four, Sir," said Omar. "Me, Sam, Sandr, and Anya."

"Four. That's reasonable. We could manage that," said Ivan. He went silent for a moment, becoming introspective, his eyes no longer focused on the group. "I'll have to work things out with a few people." Suddenly a searching look came back into his eyes, and he studied the group critically. "Is that all that you were talking about?"

"We wondered whether someone killed Father Ingall to prevent him from helping us, and whether we should expect more attacks to come," said Omar.

"You are a bright young man, Omar. Yes, we need to be cautious. If this is the start of more violent attempts to keep y'all from re-entering society, more trouble may be coming soon. Rest assured that I have seen to the security of this facility myself. It is a fortress."

"Can it withstand a mob?" asked Sam.

"Yes. You have only to retreat to the center of the building. The cafeteria is the best panic room money can buy. The various layers of protection, including fire-retardant systems, air filtration, and barricades that I've had installed, will protect you."

"I'm ready to get out of this building, Sir," Omar said.

"I know. Have just a little more patience. They may have killed Father Ingall, but shooting the messenger won't change the message. The solution Dr. Park came up with will work. We will be announcing it to the public after the funeral. The announcement would have gone more smoothly with Father Ingall, but we can and will proceed without him."

Sam, Sandr, and Anya looked reassured, but the wary concern in Omar's eyes didn't fade. They were still facing an uphill battle against public opinion.

As her father spoke, Elizaveta spotted another teenager entering the room in the flood of arriving family members. She slipped away from her father's side to join him.

"Did you get more paint?" she asked, whispering in the boy's ear from behind his left shoulder.

The dark-haired boy, with a nose still too big for his face, turned his head minutely in the direction of her voice, but didn't turn around to look at her. He glanced around the crowded room before he whispered an answer. "Yes, but don't ask me now. Omar is watching. He thinks I shouldn't get involved. We'll discuss it later. I know a spot where it will be most visible. We can go tonight. I'll pick you up at the usual place."

Karim Yassine, the sixteen-year-old brother of Omar, was tired of all the talk about patience. He wanted Omar released immediately, before some insane public official decided to castrate him or send him to an adult prison. Karim would do anything in his power to help his brother.

With her bright blue eyes shining, Elizaveta directed a look of admiration at the curling locks on the back of Karim's dark head, before sliding back to her father's side.

The room filled with conversation and laughter as the evening visitation period progressed.

∾

DRIVING THROUGH HOUSTON was gray and somber, befitting Nate's mood. The city suffered from an abundance of gray concrete and steel, which could combine with cloud cover to produce a somber effect. Graffiti covered the sides of some bridges, and crews worked to scrub it off brick walls, electrical transformers, and buildings. The stylized writing would reappear almost as soon as it was cleaned up, as the rival gangs behind the markings vied for control of their respective areas. It wasn't until Nate got stuck in traffic under an overpass on I-10 that he realized he could read some of the graffiti. Instead of illegible, stylized words, he saw bold block capital letters announcing "FREE THE CHILDREN NOW!" Startled, he began to watch more closely and found four more instances of graffiti calling for the children's freedom before he reached the exit to Gessner Road. In at least one place, the painter would have had to hang from a rope to scrawl the words that were five feet tall in the middle of a thirty-foot section of a concrete retaining wall. Someone had taken quite a risk.

Inside the hospital lobby, Nate spied the information desk and approached the young man sitting there. Before Nate had crossed the length of the lobby, the man had looked Nate over carefully. Nate realized that this wasn't the usual hospital volunteer. He was too alert to his surroundings, and he was actively scanning the lobby. He struck Nate as more of a well-trained security specialist than a receptionist.

"I'm here to see Dr. Willett King. He said he would put my name on the list of visitors," Nate said to the young man. Looking the receptionist over more closely, Nate decided he was armed, too. Definitely not your average candy striper.

"May I see some identification, please?" the receptionist-guard inquired.

Nate pulled his license out of his wallet and handed it to the man. The man compared Nate's name to the one on his list and scanned the license to make sure it wasn't a fake. *"Quite a bit more security than one usually finds in a hospital lobby,"* Nate thought.

When he was satisfied with Nate's identification, the man said, "Take the East elevators to the fourth floor, turn right, and follow the corridor to suite 485."

Suite 485 was an office suite with unlabeled glass doors. The other offices Nate had passed on the way to 485 bore names of clinics, specializations, departments, or individual doctors on the doors. On closer examination, he could see that words had been removed from 485.

Pulling the door open, Nate walked into a small outer office with an unattended desk. More offices looked to be hidden down a short hallway behind the desk.

"Hello? Dr. King?" he called out.

A gray-bearded, white-haired man in an old-fashioned white lab coat with "Dr. Willett King" stitched over the right breast came out of one of the rooms. He extended his hand to greet Nate.

"Mr. Bryan, I'm pleased to meet you. Your brother's death is a blow to us all. He was a great voice of reason and a compelling advocate for the children. I will miss him terribly," said the doctor in a sober, nasal-tinged voice.

"Thank you. As I mentioned before, I'd really like to hear about your work for the children and how Ingall was involved. Were you working on a cure for the children?"

"Not exactly. In the first years after the condition was identified, a lot of the best minds in the country focused on ways to engineer a fix or treatment for the children, since the problem was found to be linked to a specific gene mutation. However, despite a myriad of approaches to the problem, no one was successful. None of the proposed solutions got beyond animal testing. However, in my lab, we were able to induce the effects of the mutations, identifying the switches activated by the gene in question. We'd hoped that, by learning the activation mechanism, we would be able to reverse it as well. In spite of our best efforts, none of the solutions we devised came to fruition."

"So the research is at a standstill?" asked Nate, puzzled. "I thought a solution was found."

"No, no. We have a solution, but it isn't a cure. I'll get to that in a moment. First, you said on the phone that you didn't think the police are working to solve Father Ingall's murder. What makes you think that?"

"The detective in charge, his name is Janwari, lost family in an incident involving an Allergen Child. He hates the children and thinks they are a public menace. I think he might sympathize too much with the murderer to want to pursue the investigation properly. He could simply let the case go cold."

The doctor's cheeks took on a flush. "I see. So you decided to investigate the matter yourself. What experience do you have in investigating a murder?"

"None at all. I just can't let it rest."

The doctor nodded. "Well, then, I'm not sure what you can do to solve the case. But I'll tell you about our research. One of the other researchers here had an idea that we think has great potential to solve the problem of the children outright. The solution is unusual and innovative and requires some rethinking. Knee-jerk opposition is sure to arise. We hope that, in the end, the logic of the answer will win out."

"Can you tell me about it?"

"We can. I'm sure you'll appreciate the roadblocks ahead of us once we explain the matter. But first, let me call Dr. Park in to explain. The idea is hers. She's been working for the last year toward getting approval to test her solution in human trials. One week ago, she was approved to go to human trials!" He picked up an extension on the desk, dialed, and spoke a few quick words before ending the conversation. "She'll be here momentarily."

"Ingall's assistant said he was excited about this solution."

"Yes, Father Ingall had agreed to help us present the solution to the media. Dr. Park is preparing a paper for the medical community, but it's highly technical in nature, not at the reading level of the average man on the street. Father Ingall was going to present the solution to the population through the news media. He was writing an article to be published online and planned to do interviews with all the major news networks. I'm not a good public speaker. When I describe the research, I tend to fall into the minutiae of the problem at a subcellular level. The public doesn't want to hear about receptors and enzyme reactions. They want the big picture. Dr. Park is better at such things, so she was supposed to stand alongside Father Ingall during the announcement."

"Ingall was going to help present the solution to the public?"

"Yes. He was a gifted speaker. But more than that, he was going to lead the way. He volunteered for the human trial. We were discussing whether to do the trial first and then go public with the results, or to explain the issue to the public first so that the media could follow the trial as it progressed."

"Ingall volunteered for the trial? What did that involve? He didn't carry the mutation. How could *he* help?" asked Nate in confusion. As Nate asked his question, the door behind him opened. He turned to see a petite woman of mixed Asian and Caucasian ancestry come into the room. She was lovely, with green, almond-shaped eyes; delicate, pale skin across flat cheeks; and long, silky, light-brown hair.

"Dr. Park, thank you for joining us. This is Mr. Nate Bryan, Father Ingall Bryan's brother. Mr. Bryan, this is Dr. Micaela Park."

Nate stood and shook her hand. Her fingers were smooth and cool to the touch, but her shake was firm. She smiled politely, although with a look of curiosity on her face.

"I'm pleased to meet you, Mr. Bryan. I can't tell you how sorry I am about your brother's death. He was a valuable friend and the most ethically and morally grounded person I've ever met. He was instinctively kind to those in need and driven to help. He wasn't one to sit and watch when there was work to be done."

Her words came almost as if she were challenging Nate, her eyes evaluating his reaction as she spoke. She was watching him for something, but he didn't know what yet.

"Dr. King was about to tell me about the solution you developed for the Allergen Children. Could you tell me about it?" Nate waited until she sat down before resuming his own seat.

She looked at Dr. King, and he nodded for her to go ahead with her explanation.

"Well, the solution isn't exactly for the children. It's for everyone else." She watched for Nate's reaction.

Nate's eyebrows went up. "Go on."

"We can't undo the condition in the children, but that may not be a bad thing. As you know, because of their mutations, the children exude a secretion that can cause a dangerous allergic reaction in other people who don't carry at least a single copy of the mutation. As near as we can tell, about sixty-five to seventy-five percent of the population does not carry the mutation, a large percentage, but not as high as the initial eighty-percent estimates. However, we've discovered that the mutation has a number of medical benefits. Those carrying even the single mutation don't have dietary, medicinal, or environmental allergies of any kind. Their immune systems do not overreact in the way other people's can. Consequently, they don't suffer from any autoimmune diseases. They have no allergies, no asthma, no rheumatoid arthritis, no lupus, no multiple sclerosis, no psoriasis, nor any other condition involving an overreaction of the immune system. In essence, the mutation is a cure for all of those conditions, and we have discovered how to induce the physiological reactions caused by the mutation. We can cure all of those conditions!"

Nate's head reeled slightly as he considered what she was saying. "The solution, then, isn't to cure the children, but to give everyone else the same condition. Would they produce the toxic skin oils, too? How would you do it?"

"It works like a vaccination. We expect booster shots will be needed every ten years for safety. The people with the induced version of the single mutation shouldn't excrete toxin in their skin oil. If we give everyone the equivalent to a single mutation, they'll all be immune to the toxin. Carriers of the double mutation will be able to rejoin the population safely."

"So you'd eventually hope to give the vaccination to newborns? Protecting the whole population?" said Nate.

"For generations, yes. After that, I expect they'd test in utero and give shots only to those who need them. Consider the long-term view. Over time, the mutation will continue to spread as people who carry it have children. People with the mutation have been identified on every single continent. In some parts of the world, up to thirty-five percent of the population is thought to carry a single copy of the mutation. Over time, fewer and fewer people will need the vaccination as more and more are born with the mutation. On top of the lack of autoimmune disorders, we've seen no instances of cancer in children who carry the mutation. When viruses move through the camps, the children recover in a fraction of the time it takes the staff and families. We feel the children represent a medical advance for humanity." She was still watching Nate's face, trying to read his reaction.

He could see why she was wary. The information was staggering. "Then the problem wasn't linked to that allergy medicine?"

"That medicine was sold over the counter as an antihistamine ointment for skin rashes in some parts of the globe for more than seventy years. Its main ingredient is a plant extract used by native peoples for centuries. Various subspecies of the plant are found on three continents. I doubt we'll ever be able to say definitively whether that medicine was a factor or not. The prevalence of the mutation is higher in places where the plant is found, but all of those places are also petroleum-producing countries. Both factors could be involved, or the cause may be some unidentified factor. It's unlikely that we'll ever know for sure. Establishing a causal relationship between any single substance or combination of substances and a known change at the genetic level is, at this point, impossible. Focusing on the origins of the mutation is, in my opinion, a waste of time. Given the benefits of the mutation, natural selection may be playing a part in its increasing prevalence. I prefer to focus on what this issue will look like globally in the future."

Nate hadn't thought about the world view, but the knee-jerk reaction to Dr. Park's information in the United States could be frightening. The prospect of asking people to trust the doctors to give them a condition that they saw as deadly was mind-boggling at best. Even as a treatment to cure all of those other conditions, it might be a hard sell. At the same time, the light of logic was furiously proclaiming to Nate that this was a real answer for the children as well as an advance for the population as a whole. He understood why Ingall had volunteered for the trial. He saw why Ingall had spoken of paths. Ingall had made his choice.

"Your brother once told me that he thought his twin would love our labs here. He said you were a biochemistry professor in San Marcos, but that you used to do research and development for the pharmaceutical industry. Why did you switch to teaching, Dr. Bryan? It is Doctor, isn't it?"

Dr. Park's green eyes held Nate's. She was an intense and focused person. He wasn't sure he enjoyed being the subject of her scrutiny. All the same, he thought she was probably one hell of a researcher. "Yes, it's Dr. Bryan, but Nate will do. I became disenchanted with the industry," he said, knowing she would require more data but waiting for her to ask for it.

"Why?"

"I won't say which company or which drugs, but I was frustrated by the company's push to replace medications that worked well with new ones that didn't work as well simply because their patents were expiring. When I reached the point that it felt like my work was doing more harm than good, I called it quits and went back to academia."

"Why didn't you switch areas of research? Move to a different company? Or, better yet, why didn't you come to work with your brother? We need top researchers."

Nate grappled for an answer. Dr. Park had gone straight to the heart of the matter. "From my contacts in the industry, I knew that my frustrations were common to researchers in all of the companies. Why I didn't switch areas is more complicated. You are a researcher. You understand how the process works, and you understand the inherent problems in the way research is done. Because of the complex interactions between systems in the body, pulling a reaction or chain of reactions out to study in a lab environment doesn't give a true picture of what really happens in the body. The complexities of the systems make unforeseen interactions a life-or-death matter."

Nate could see the light go on in Dr. Park's eyes. Again, she read between the lines, seeing through his generalization. "A drug you created failed in trials because of an unforeseen interaction. Were there deaths?"

"Yes."

"So you fell off the horse and decided not to get back on? What did Father Ingall think of that choice?"

"He knew I needed time."

"How long have you been teaching now?"

"Five years."

"Hmm," she said, the intense look on her facing softening to sadness.

Nate knew what she was thinking. Her unexpressed thought hung in the air in the room. For months he'd had a nagging feeling that a new project was waiting for him in a corner of his mind, if only he'd think about it. His dreams had been filled with an idea that he knew would coalesce into something solid if he were to give it half the chance. But teaching had become comfortable. He knew Dr. Park could see that he was sitting on the sidelines, choosing not to re-enter the game.

Nate thought about Dr. Park's upcoming trial. The possibility for unforeseen interactions loomed over it. Ingall had volunteered knowing the process, knowing how pharmaceutical studies worked. Even if the study were to make it past the trial phase, convincing the population that the treatment was good for them would be difficult. Disseminating misinformation online was too easy. Once opposition forces dug in, the lies would spread like wildfire. Antitreatment efforts would rise. Overcoming that reaction would take work, patience, and years of effort. The road forward would be rocky at best, but it had a real chance of succeeding, given all the people who could be cured of other conditions with the treatment.

"Thank you for meeting with me. You've given me a lot to consider. When do you plan to announce the trials to the media? Ingall left a cryptic note about announcing your solution," said Nate, turning to Dr. King and away from Dr. Park's intense eyes.

"We would have held a news conference this week. We may still do so after Father Ingall's funeral," said Dr. King.

"Let me know if I can be of any assistance," said Nate as he stood to leave and shook Dr. King's hand. He forced himself to nod goodbye to Dr. Park and shake her hand firmly. Nate thought Dr. Park looked disappointed as he left. She had to know he wasn't Ingall and could never do what Ingall could have done. What had she expected him to say? Did she expect him to drop everything and go into research with her? If he were ever to go back to research, which was still not a certainty in his mind, he wasn't sure he would want to jump right into her lab.

Back in his hotel room, Nate sat on his bed and read news articles. A congressman had proposed requiring couples to be screened for the Allergen gene mutation with every pregnancy. The representative had argued that the Rh factor for both parents was determined for births, that HIV status was tested, and that, given the danger the mutation posed to society, testing for it should be required, too. He wanted testing done early in the pregnancy so that parents could opt to abort.

The idea of encouraging people to abort perfectly healthy kids—kids who were healthier than the rest of the population and who might be more medically advanced than everyone else—made Nate ill. The congressman, on the other hand, had framed it as an act of mercy, to save the children from growing up in camps, separated from their families, with no prospects for the future. Nate doubted that the congressman was really concerned about the welfare of the children. His main interest was, as usual, the bottom line for the state and nation. It was costing the state a fortune to house and raise the kids in quarantine. The senator would rather people choose to abort than spend any more tax money on the children.

Society always did what was expedient over what was right, especially if what was right took effort or cost money. The bulk of society would turn a blind eye to the problem for as long as possible, feeling that if it didn't affect them individually, they need not be concerned about it. That same sort of thinking had led to the Holocaust.

Nate shut down the tablet he was reading and went to take a shower. He felt dirty by association, as a member of society who had needed Ingall to help him see the wrong around him. Now, Ingall was gone. Who would make the rest of society see the wrong?

Chapter 3

Tuesday morning after breakfast, Nate found himself facing Ivan Tolokonsky in a well-appointed but not ostentatious house situated off Memorial Drive. Given Tolokonsky's known wealth, Nate had expected a mansion. By comparison to his expectations, the five-bedroom, four-thousand-square-foot home was modest.

"Thank you for seeing me," Nate said as they shook hands.

Tolokonsky was fifty-one years old, blond with blue eyes and tanned skin. Nate had researched his biography before driving over and could see the former oil-field safety worker under the clothing of the business executive. Tolokonsky gave Nate the impression of being a man with the boundless energy and endless persistence of all inventors. He had designed more than five hundred other methods for replacing hydraulic fracturing on paper before he'd discovered the perfect one. Once he'd made his fortune, he had planned to revamp other areas of petroleum engineering. However, when his children's condition came to light, Tolokonsky changed his focus to helping his children and improving the lives of all the children in the camps. Tolokonsky owned the patent on his oil-extraction process and owned the largest company in the United States that was selling equipment to extract oil from shale, but he left the day-to-day operations of the company to an appointed CEO and board of directors.

When his children had first been quarantined, Ivan and his wife, Vera, had spent every day at the quarantine facility with them, fighting for space for them to be a family. They had tried to give the children a home life in the camp, eating meals with them, reading them bedtime stories, bathing them, clothing them, and teaching them when they had been small. As the children had grown and no medical answers had appeared, the issue of schooling had arisen. Vera had taught the children herself while Ivan had pushed for a regular school to be created within the camp. Once the school had been organized, Ivan had pushed for higher standards, while Vera had organized extracurricular activities, such as chess teams and drama clubs. They had fought to allow the children to have pets, campfires, and other experiences that they had been denied because of their enforced quarantine. Ivan and Vera had spent their own money and raised funds for sports facilities, pools, theaters, art supplies, and musical instruments. They'd dedicated themselves to preparing their children and the others in the camp for the day when they would be allowed to rejoin society, while simultaneously funding and lobbying for research to cure the children's condition.

Nate respected Ivan and Vera for their work and dedication, but knew Ivan was a hard man to like personally. He was a bulldozer, clearing obstacles by any means necessary, stepping on toes and not caring whose feelings he hurt as he went.

"Mr. Bryan, you look a little like your brother," Tolokonsky said as he opened the door to greet Nate. "I can see it in the shape of your nose and mouth. Please accept my condolences."

"Thank you," said Nate, thinking his only real likeness to his brother had been their matching receding hairlines. Others had seen a family resemblance between them, but Nate had never been able to see it.

Tolokonsky directed Nate to sit on a cream-colored suede couch in a living room that could have been taken right out of a magazine. Subtle creams, yellows, and pale blues blended to create a comfortable but elegant space. Tile floors shone in the morning sunlight. The area rug beneath their feet was soft and intricately patterned.

"Mr. Tolokonsky, could you tell me what you saw Ingall about earlier this week? I know he was expecting trouble, based on a message I received from him. However, he didn't specify the problem. Did you know of any threats he'd received?"

Tolokonsky looked chagrined. He sighed and said, "Father Ingall received threats all the time because he believed my children should be allowed to live freely in society. I offered him protection. I wanted him to have a bodyguard, but he refused. I should simply have assigned someone to protect him without telling him. He need not have died."

"The police will review all the threats Ingall received, but I'm concerned that they may not really want his murder solved."

"What makes you say that?" asked Tolokonsky, an intent look and a hint of anger sparking in his eyes.

"The detective in charge of the case called the Allergen Children 'born killers.' He apparently lost family in an incident involving an Allergen Child."

"Damn! I suppose I shouldn't be surprised. The official line has never been favorable to the children. Those who help them are probably equally suspect in the eyes of law enforcement. I take it that you have decided to investigate for yourself. What do you want me to do?"

"Right now I need information. Can you think of anyone who would go so far as to murder Ingall? Anyone he would have agreed to meet with at night? Based on a message I got from him, Ingall knew he might have been in trouble before he died. He was meeting someone he knew was dangerous, but he did it anyway. I know he'd tried to speak to Landon Piccone, but Piccone had refused. People who gave Ingall a chance to speak to them, especially those who had threatened him, typically backed down and at least agreed to disagree. He wasn't afraid of them. Do you think he might have been trying to speak to Piccone? Can you think of anyone else he might have agreed to speak to but distrusted?"

At the mention of Piccone, the expression on Tolokonsky's face hardened. "That man is a moron. Father Ingall kept reminding me that he grieves the loss of his children, but he is still a moron. Piccone is adept at filing legal papers, but he lacks physical courage. The one time we almost came face to face at a conference two years ago, he turned and fled the room rather than meet me in person without a lawyer between us. He is a spineless coward who won't listen, learn, or consider hard science." The anger and contempt in Tolokonsky's voice made it deep and heavy, laden with emotion. "However, because he is a coward, I can't see him killing Father Ingall. Someone else did that. The one I'd like to question is Piccone's fourteen-year-old daughter, Jeanette. She's a spitfire with no fear. She came up to me once and called me a murderer to my face. She spat at me and would have slapped me if someone hadn't pulled her away." His voice softened with respect for the girl's courage.

"At fourteen, she would have needed help to get to Ingall, someone to drive her, get her a weapon, help her flee the scene," Nate said, surprised at the respect in Tolokonsky's voice.

"She has a boyfriend who is sixteen who shares her ideology. He lost a parent." Here, Ivan's voice was neutral. He had no opinion of the boyfriend as of yet, Nate guessed.

"Why would they kill Ingall now?" asked Nate.

"Because he was on the brink of championing a solution that would result in freeing the children. As long as the children are quarantined, without freedom, the Piccones feel a measure of justice for their loss. If my children become free to live their lives, that measure of justice vanishes. Piccone can't seem to comprehend that my children did nothing wrong, that it was all a terrible accident. I recognize his pain and loss, but we do not live in an 'eye-for-an-eye' society."

"Do you think Dr. Park's solution will work? Will people be willing to be vaccinated to become like your children?" asked Nate.

"With your brother leading by example, yes, we could have won over the bulk of the people, perhaps even quickly. The science stands for itself. We will gain many supporters when those who suffer from chronic autoimmune disorders join us. The parents of children with uncontrolled asthma and juvenile rheumatoid arthritis will jump at a cure. People with family histories of certain cancers that are genetically based would come, too. Convincing people who don't have a stake in the matter will be harder, without people like Father Ingall, who are willing to lead by example. If we can counter the shouts of those unwilling to take the science as fact, in the end, the majority of the people will understand the benefits of the vaccine. At least, that is my hope. Certainly, it will take longer without Father Ingall's help."

"Is Mr. Piccone aware of Dr. Park's idea yet? Does he know that the doctors have found a way for the children to be free?"

"I don't know what he knows. We think he has people feeding him information from within the hospital. The doctors suspect someone at the hospital of helping Piccone's people, but we don't know how much information they get. Vandals got into the offices and broke things, scattered papers, and scrawled hateful words on the walls when the doctors were out. The doctors thought whoever did that must have had inside help, since the door lock wasn't broken. Someone got hold of a key. They've increased security at the hospital and added biometric locks to the doors because of that incident."

"When did that happen?"

"About six months ago."

Nate nodded. If Piccone's people had been leaked information about the treatment Dr. Park had created, someone could have decided to try to block its progress by stopping Ingall from leading the way in a trial of the treatment. People would have listened to Ingall and trusted him. He'd had that quality about him that had made people believe in him and the truth of his words. Lots of people didn't trust doctors, scientists, or the government, and believed that all those sources would lie to them. Ingall had been a different story. He had been too trustworthy, and his motives too pure. People could not have disbelieved him any more than they could have disbelieved or distrusted Mother Teresa of Calcutta in her day. The opposition might have hoped that stopping Ingall from championing the trial could set the trial back for years, or even indefinitely.

"Is that what you saw Ingall about this week, the trials of the treatment?" Nate asked.

"No, I asked Father Ingall to go see my children in the camp, to counsel them. Some of the older children in the camps are getting restless. They are young and spirited. They lack patience."

"Is rebellion a possibility?"

"Not merely a possibility. They are ready to resist any efforts to imprison or sterilize them. Around the country, some of the teenagers have finished their education, and I don't mean only through high school. Several already have bachelor's degrees from online university programs. Some of them have more than one degree. With so little freedom and so much controlled time spent on education in the camps, the children, even working at their own pace, outstrip regular schools. They complete subjects quickly and move on to the next. They want to start careers, drive cars, travel. One such young person in Louisiana wants to go to medical school and has passed the exams necessary to enter. These young people only lack the freedom they need to meet their goals. They are frustrated. Frustration leads to rebellion."

"How was Ingall handling it?"

"He advised nonviolent protests, pointing out that the children would hurt their cause if people feared them even more than they already do. He let them know that he was with them, working for them all the time. He went to tell them that Dr. Park's treatment plan had been approved for trials last week."

"So the children have been kept apprised of the progress?"

"Yes. They are cautiously optimistic about being released. They can see the pitfalls ahead. They're worried it may all come to nothing. They aren't naïve. They know people fear them. The talk in the media right now is quite extreme, especially the calls for sterilization. The children are looking for a way to show people that they are human beings, not mutant monsters."

"Do you think I could meet your children? I'd like to visit the camps and see the state of things for myself. I know I can't take Ingall's place, but I would like to help."

"The children would probably like to meet you, too. They will want to express their condolences personally. Four of the oldest want to attend the funeral. I'm working to make that happen right now, but I know they would be pleased by the gesture if you went to see them. Thank you for your interest in them. I will call the camps and let them know that you have my permission to speak to my children," said Mr. Tolokonsky. "We are hoping that the reporters will want to speak to the children after the funeral and put them on the news. Giving them faces in the eyes of the public with help their cause."

"Ingall would probably be happy to be of service, even in death," said Nate.

Mr. Tolokonsky said, "Exactly." Nate could see that Tolokonsky assumed Nate would agree to this use of his brother's funeral for publicity. Tolokonsky wasn't asking for permission. He was stating what he was going to do. Nate was sure that, had he disagreed, Tolokonsky would have proceeded as planned without apology.

"How are the conditions in the camps right now? You and your wife have worked hard to make life as normal as possible for the children. Have you succeeded in creating a homelike atmosphere?" Nate asked, deciding to shift the topic.

"Everything was almost perfect until about eighteen months ago. Things are changing in ominous ways. Doors that were never locked during the day are now locked as a matter of course. Places that used to have receptionists now have guards. Cameras have been added. Some of the changes were necessary to protect the children from attack from the outside, but the children realize that some of it is to keep them inside as well. They used to have freedom to wander the camps, moving from gyms to computer rooms to lounges to cafeterias freely. The atmosphere was homelike. Now they have to get permission and be escorted. Monitoring has become constant. Razor wire was added to the fences. The whole compound is becoming less of a camp and more of a fortress. I have overseen and paid for the security improvements needed to protect my children from an outside assault. The internal restrictions on the children's movements as well as the monitoring have been implemented by the county and state health departments and by various federal agencies. My children are uneasy about these changes. My daughter Anya suffers from anxiety and has trouble sleeping at night. My son, Oleksandr, is angry and frustrated." The anger in Tolokonsky's face lit his eyes with heat and pulsed in the muscles of his jaw. Nate could see that he would mount an armed defense of his children without hesitation.

"What do you think caused these changes?" asked Nate.

"I think the lawmakers suddenly realized how old the children are. How close to adulthood. A locked-up child isn't a threat to anyone. A locked-up adult, on the other hand, can be a threat. Whenever rules have been changed in a way that restricts the children, the People's Health and Safety League has usually been behind the change, typically with some petition signed by fools convinced that they have to protect society from my children." A sneer formed on Tolokonsky's face as he mentioned the group organized by Landon Piccone.

At that moment, a lovely teenager in skintight jeans, leather half boots, and a sleeveless shirt charged into the room. Her blue eyes matched her father's in shape, but her beautiful button nose and pointed chin must have come from her mother.

"Daddy, have you seen the . . ." She skidded to a stop, and her words trailed off as she noticed Nate's presence.

"Mr. Bryan, this is my daughter, Elizaveta. Eliza, my dear, this is Father Ingall's brother." The sneer that had been on the man's face vanished and was replaced by a look of pleasure.

"Hello, Mr. Bryan." She glanced at her father, and he nodded encouragement at her. She reached a hand forward to shake.

Nate shook her thin hand and gave her a smile. A strip of pink hair fell down by her right ear amid the rest of her straight blonde hair. Large geometric earrings dangled from her ears down to her shoulders. She looked to be about fourteen, but was wearing thick, dark mascara, bright pink lipstick, and too much rouge in an attempt to appear older. Her immature figure proclaimed her youth.

"Pleased to meet you," Nate said.

"We were sorry to hear about your brother. They'd better catch whoever killed him! He was so nice to me. He worked so hard to help Anya and Sandr." Tears formed at the corners of her eyes, but she brushed them away, took a deep breath, and controlled herself.

Her father put his arm around her shoulders and squeezed her to his side briefly before releasing her with a kiss to her temple.

"We will have to work harder now that Father Ingall is gone. They can't stop us," she said. Determination and the same spark of anger Nate had seen in her father's eyes filled hers as the pointed chin came up defiantly.

"Yes, my dear," said her father, pride highlighting the smile twitching on his lips.

"Will we go to the camp today?" she asked her father.

"Tomorrow. We're taking your grandmother's blini for an evening treat."

She nodded and pushed the pink strand of hair back behind her right ear. As she lowered her hand, Nate noticed that her pinkie finger was stained black on the outer edge and her index finger was black on the tip. She'd been handling some kind of paint. On her forearm, an old bruise tinted the skin green and yellow.

Vera Tolokonsky entered the room. Shorter than her daughter but with the same pixie nose and chin set between wide cheekbones, Mrs. Tolokonsky looked intelligent but troubled. Classically dressed in a pale-pink silk blouse and perfectly tailored black slacks over a slender figure with black, low-heeled shoes, she extended a hand to greet Nate.

"Mr. Bryan, I'm Vera Tolokonsky. I'm pleased to meet you. Please accept my condolences on your loss. We will miss you brother terribly."

Although her face looked as unlined as her daughter's, Vera Tolokonsky's hands revealed her age. Blue veins bulged along the backs of her hands, which were as small as her daughter's but decked in rings. The skin over her knuckles was pale and deeply wrinkled. Nate guessed her to be in her upper forties.

"Thank you, Ma'am."

"Please sit down," she said, extending a graceful arm toward the couch Nate had vacated when her daughter had entered the room.

"Mom, I've got things to do. I need to go," said Elizaveta, backing slowly away from the adults and out of the room. She held her phone in her left hand and waved it at her mother.

Her mother gave her an exasperated look but nodded, while her father gave her a fond smile and made shooing motions, flicking his hands to dismiss her. The teenager turned and fled the room.

"Mrs. Tolokonsky, other than Mr. Piccone, can you think of anyone my brother had had trouble with recently, any kind of conflict or personal problems?" Nate began.

"Father Ingall must have received as many death threats as we do," she said, with an anxious glance at her husband. She gripped her hands together in her lap, digging the long acrylic nails of one hand into the back of the other, leaving tiny half-moon indentations in her skin.

"The police are reviewing those," Nate said, "but I wanted to know if he'd had any more personal conflicts, perhaps with someone he knew, someone he worked with, maybe at the camps or in fundraising?"

A delicate blush rose to her cheeks. She glanced at her husband again. "We had some disagreements on the course we should take to fight for the children's rights. Father Ingall agreed with picketing the legislature, giving speeches, and other nonviolent protests. My husband's methods weren't always what Father Ingall could condone. We feel we need to get votes against the various laws being recommended by any means necessary. My husband has hired private investigators to look into the lives of some of the legislators, in hopes of acquiring leverage that might help us convince them to vote in our favor. In other instances, we think the support we need might be gained for a price."

"Extortion and bribery? Ingall would have balked at that." Nate gave her an encouraging smile that he hoped projected understanding for their plight. He didn't want to appear judgmental, even though he felt their methods would backfire on them.

"We had some heated arguments over the subject," said Mr. Tolokonsky. "I'll be candid with you, Mr. Bryan, because I know you could never prove anything against me. In the end, I decided to pursue whatever courses I could without advising Father Ingall." His voice was fierce and low, giving the impression of a man who didn't like to be crossed.

"You went behind his back then?" Nate put the question lightly, without censure, treading carefully. He wondered if this were what it felt like to question a mafia don. Obviously, Tolokonsky had money, power, and resources that he wouldn't hesitate to use in any way he felt was necessary to help his children.

"As far as I know, he never found out. I had hoped he'd thought we had dropped the ideas, but we needed to take action. If the laws being suggested are passed . . . Well, we will not stand for it. Best to stop them before they are implemented," said Mr. Tolokonsky, matching Nate's light tone on a topic that he clearly didn't take lightly.

Knowing Ingall, Nate thought, he was probably aware that the Tolokonskys were going against his advice. If he'd come across evidence, he'd probably have confronted them with it, but Nate didn't think they would kill Ingall for it. That didn't mean they hadn't killed Ingall for trying to prevent them from taking a more aggressive course to free their children. The anxiety had left Mrs. Tolokonsky's face. She wasn't worried about confiding in Nate about bribery or extortion. What, then, had made her anxious when he had started asking her questions? Nate tried again.

"Do you know if Father Ingall had any trouble recently that didn't relate to how best to help the children? Any more *personal* issues?" Nate used Ingall's shorthand for the one-sided entanglements he sometimes encountered, to see if she would recognize the term.

The blush returned to Mrs. Tolokonsky's cheeks. "I don't know," she said.

Nate thought she wasn't telling the truth.

"I don't think Father Ingall had much of a personal life. He spent so much time working that I don't think he even had any particular friends. I knew he had a twin brother because he'd mentioned you, but I'm not aware of any other family he had. I imagine you know those details better than we would," said Mr. Tolokonsky, without the slightest hint of personal concern. "If you find you need help in your investigation, anything at all, let me know. I'll be happy to assist you. I have one or two friends in law enforcement who are favorable to our cause."

"Thank you. I'll keep that in mind." said Nate.

Mrs. Tolokonsky's hands were still tightly grasped in her lap. Ivan Tolokonsky's eyes were firmly on Nate, not glancing at his wife. Her eyes kept darting to his face and back to Nate's. She knew something that she didn't want to discuss in front of her husband. Maybe Nate could get her on the phone by herself later.

Standing to leave, Nate said, "Thank you for speaking to me today. You can count on my support for the treatment the doctors have created." Nate put out a hand to shake, and Mr. Tolokonsky grasped it. "Here's my number," Nate said as he handed his business card to Mrs. Tolokonsky. "If you think of anything else, please call me. I look forward to meeting your children."

Nate drove back toward his hotel with plenty on his mind. Mrs. Tolokonsky knew something about Ingall that he suspected was personal. Based on his research, the issue of the children's rights was about to explode in the public consciousness. Which way public sentiment would go, either in favor of or against, was unknown. Whichever side was able to sway public sentiment would have the upper hand once the news of the treatment was released. Bringing a human face to the children's plight would help. Nate hoped Tolokonsky would bring his children to the funeral.

As he drove, Nate changed his mind about returning to the hotel. The obvious next move was to visit the children's camp. Ingall had described the camps to him in much the same way as Mr. Tolokonsky had: homelike facilities to make life as normal as possible for the children, sort of like a boarding school. Nate hadn't been aware of the recent changes in security. He needed to interview the teenagers for himself, to see the people Ingall knew at the camps, the doctors, and other staff workers. He wasn't looking forward to going into a place where the touch of one child could kill him, but if Ingall could do it regularly, surely Nate could do it once.

As he pulled into a twenty-four-hour pharmacy parking lot to look up directions to the camp, his phone rang.

Nate answered through the car's Bluetooth function without looking at the caller identification. "Hello?"

"Nate. I need to talk to you about Ingall's work." Loriana's husky voice filled the car. "Please, can we meet for lunch?" Nate's ears detected a note of pleading.

CHAPTER 4

Completely taken aback, he stared at the steering wheel, wondering what to say.

"Nate, are you there? Please say something."

"I'm here. Where are you?"

"I'm in Houston."

Her answer surprised him. She worked in the capitol building in downtown Austin and commuted to her home in south Austin. Nate lived in the northern part of San Marcos. When they had been dating, he had driven to Austin to see her.

"Why?"

"I was supposed to meet Ingall the night he died, but he never showed up."

"What?" Nate exclaimed.

"Look, I don't want to talk about this on the phone. Can we meet somewhere? A restaurant?"

"Why not the police station? They'll want your statement."

"I wanted to see you first. My work is involved."

Nate relented. "Okay. Fine. Where do you want to meet?"

They settled on Mexican food at noon. He suggested El Real on Westheimer in the Montrose area. El Real wasn't too far from the South Freeway, which he needed to take to get to the camps.

Driving to the restaurant, Nate experienced a range of emotions appropriate for an acting class. Alternately angry, excited, bemused, anxious, suspicious, and determined to be stoical, he still wanted to see Loriana. Kicking himself mentally, he reviewed the reasons he'd called off the wedding. The reasons were still valid. Nothing had changed. But a little part of his brain suggested that maybe something *had* changed. Maybe Loriana had changed. The silly grin that covered his face as he thought about Loriana possibly changing her mind made him feel like a lovesick puppy. He called himself to order again. Religion had been a primary bone of contention between them. Nothing she'd said indicated a change of position on that. By the time he arrived at the restaurant, he felt he might be able to face her as a reasonable, thinking human being instead of an overwrought idiot.

He walked in the door of the restaurant and saw her waiting for him, but not looking toward the door. She hadn't seen him enter. Loriana was as beautiful as ever. Then, she looked up to see him watching her. Her initial reaction was a smile filled with relief, but that quickly vanished and was replaced with a polite look of sympathy. She came over and hugged him quickly, then released him, offering condolences but nothing else.

"I'm so sorry, Nate."

"Thanks." Nate's mind froze up. He didn't want to be on the receiving end of sympathy. It reminded him that Ingall really was gone.

After they were seated with drinks and the waitress had left to place their orders, he said, "What's going on?"

Loriana's color rose slightly. She tucked her dark, heavy hair, worn loose and falling straight from a central part, behind her ears. Her eyes were wet, the chocolate brown shimmering, and she bit her lower lip on one side of her mouth. Nate's eyes were drawn to her slightly crooked nose, the distinguishing feature that saved her face from china-doll regularity and gave her character, and back to her lovely eyes.

Finding himself getting lost in those eyes, Nate ripped his own eyes away and looked for someplace else on which to focus. The restaurant was built in what had been an old theater. The owners projected old movies on the wall and kept the place decorated with black-and-white publicity photos of actors and actresses from a bygone era. Nate looked over Loriana's shoulder at the black-and-white Mexican movie running on the wall to keep himself from grabbing her hand. He'd seen her look of distress frequently in the past. He concentrated on the movie until she started to speak.

"I asked to see Ingall because I wanted to warn him about what's coming. You know I work for Senator Coalember. The senator is a lecherous dog, but he'd always seemed ethical in terms of his work and business connections."

"Seemed?"

"I'm getting there. Let me tell this in order," she said, forestalling his questions with one hand up. "A couple of weeks ago, Ivan Tolokonsky asked for an appointment to see the senator. You know the Tolokonskys?"

Nate nodded.

She gave him a grim, tight-lipped smile and continued. "I knew the senator's stance on the Allergen Children was to err on the side of public safety, even if it meant trampling people's rights. So I tried to put Mr. Tolokonsky off. The senator was busy and didn't want to waste time on the issue when he wasn't going to change his mind. When I told Mr. Tolokonsky that we didn't have any openings for the senator to meet with him any time soon, Mr. Tolokonsky said that if the senator didn't meet with him, no amount of public relations spin would save his career. I wasn't surprised. I figured that Tolokonsky had compromising pictures of the senator with yet another floozy. I scheduled the meeting, figuring the senator would want to know what Tolokonsky had on him."

"From what I know of the Tolokonskys, they have no scruples about assigning a private investigator to follow your boss. Dirty pictures were a good bet," Nate said.

She looked away in an evasive manner that set Nate's teeth on edge. She was withholding something. She gave that sad, tight smile again and said, "If only it had been an affair. Anyway, the meeting was for breakfast two days later, on a Thursday morning. When I came to break up the meeting in order to get the senator to his next appointment on time, I heard Mr. Tolokonsky say, 'You won't profit off the misery of our children. We have proof that will stand up in court. Either you support us in the voting, or we release the details.' The senator swept the papers off the table and stomped out of the room with his fists clenched. He didn't even see me coming to get him from the other side of the room."

"So the senator is accepting bribes. Do you know from whom?"

"As I followed the senator out, Mr. Tolokonsky stopped me and handed me a manila envelope. He said I should give it to my boss."

"Did you look in the envelope?"

"Not then. I didn't have time. I needed to get the senator to his next meeting."

"But later?"

"Later, I found the envelope in the trash and glanced at the papers inside. They were documents dealing with the construction of some kind of large facility in West Texas, about thirty miles from Van Horn, by a company called Limestone Wells Construction."

"In the middle of nowhere?"

"Yeah. I didn't see anything that suggested bribery in the envelope, so I put it back in the trash. But the whole situation irritated me, so, a few days later, I did some digging.

The owners of the company planning to build the facility in West Texas made several huge donations to the senator's re-election campaign."

"How huge?"

"Three million dollars total."

"Wow."

"But that's not the worst of it," she said, leaning forward to speak even more quietly than the husky whisper she'd been using all along.

Nate had to force himself to focus on her big brown eyes instead of the gap at the V-neck opening of the blouse she was wearing. "How does it get worse than that?"

"I found a letter in our records from Limestone Wells Construction explaining the facility's purpose: It's a high-security prison to house all of the Allergen Children from Louisiana and Texas. The senator is going to propose a law requiring that the children be moved away from high-population areas for the protection of the public. He is going to recommend that they be moved to the facility this company is building. Limestone Wells Construction will be the only company ready to supply the needs of such a law. They'll make a bundle of money off of government contracts."

"Okay. You found all this, and then you went to tell Ingall. Did you confront the senator, too?"

"I tried, but he refused to talk to me. Then I remembered he'd been meeting with the two senators from Louisiana, ostensibly to discuss regional issues. I think they've been paid off, too. The plans I saw called for moving all the children from the Chalmette and Baton Rouge facilities in Louisiana and the children from the South Houston, Baytown, and Beaumont facilities to West Texas. Their families would practically never see them, let alone be able to stay with the littlest ones overnight, like they can now." Tears filled her eyes.

Again, Loriana had surprised Nate. "Why does this matter to you?" he asked. "You never cared about the children. You said trying to fight for them was a lost cause and a waste of financial resources." He asked the question softly, as gently as he could. He didn't want to make her defensive.

"I was wrong." She brushed a tear away with the table napkin.

While Nate accepted the admission, she still hadn't told him her reasons. None of his logical arguments or ethical arguments had previously swayed her. "What changed your mind?"

"I was visiting my mom at the elder-care facility a few months ago. It was one of her better days. She recognized me and was mostly lucid and in the present. Sometimes, when I visit, she thinks it's 1980. We were watching television, and the news came on. One segment revisited the possible causes for the gene mutation—the allergy medication and exposure to petrochemicals. Suddenly, she said that my dad had taken that medicine. I never knew that my dad had allergies. I was only nine when he died in a rig accident. We moved from one petrochemical hub to another when I was little.

"Given that I fit the criteria for the mutation, I submitted a sample for genetic testing about three months ago. The results came back, and I'm a carrier. My kids or grandkids could get the double mutation if my spouse is a carrier or if one of my kids marries a carrier. The whole problem became personal." Her brown eyes, sad and glistening, held Nate's. "I'm one of those complacent idiots that history despises—those who wait 'til a problem affects them before taking an interest."

"You came around sooner than most. A lot of people don't get to the point that you're at until a child is born into their family with the double mutation." He wanted to forgive her, but, at the same time, he wanted her to be ashamed of herself.

For this, Nate berated himself mentally and thought of Ingall. Ingall would have hugged her and celebrated that she had found the truth, greeting her like the Prodigal returned. Nate bit his tongue and held back any bitter comments. A moment later, he was grateful he had held back.

"Thanks for not saying 'I told you so.' You're entitled to it. You gave me every piece of information I needed, including that supporting the children was the right thing to do, and I ignored you." She smiled with a familiar affectionate look in her eyes.

Hope stirred in Nate's chest and his heart began to beat a little faster. Nate gathered his wits and considered for a moment. "If the Tolokonskys know about this scheme and the bribery, they'll bring down your boss if he doesn't cooperate with them. You may want to consider a career move."

She laughed a deep-throated chuckle. "My letter of resignation is written and ready to be sent. But what do I do now?"

Nate considered the situation. The ramifications of the problem were complex. If the Tolokonskys were to expose the senator for accepting bribes, he could be replaced by someone equally opposed to the Children's Rights Movement. If they were not to expose the senator, they would be leaving a criminal in office who would be irked by the pressure placed on him by the Tolokonskys. Men like that, when cornered, had been known to bite back. Could the senator have killed Ingall, thinking that Ingall was helping the Tolokonskys?

"Do you know where the senator was the night Ingall died?" Nate asked.

"At a fundraiser in Dallas. He gave a speech at eight p.m. in the Convention Center and answered questions from the press at nine-thirty p.m. He was interviewed by a local morning news show this morning. He isn't scheduled to leave Dallas until this afternoon. However, that doesn't mean he didn't send someone to kill Ingall."

"Would he have gone after Ingall? The Tolokonskys seem more likely targets."

"Frankly, I don't think he would have thought in terms of murdering anyone, but then I thought he was ethical in his business practices, so what do I know? Anything is possible." Her tone was filled with exasperation and frustration with herself and with the entire situation. She was tired of trying to deal with the problem alone.

Putting aside the issue of the senator, another thought occurred to Nate. "When and where were you supposed to meet Ingall the night he died? How did you communicate with him?"

"I called him three days ago. We agreed to meet at his office at ten p.m. He had other meetings, and I was going to drive in from Austin after work, so it had to be late."

"The police will check his phone records and see that you spoke. They'll be contacting you. You may want to go to them before they come to you. It might look better if you did."

"Meaning they might be suspicious if I don't?" She raised an eyebrow at him.

"Yes."

"If he was already dead by ten p.m., I'll be cleared."

"Ingall died at 1:26 a.m.," Nate said, watching for her response.

She stared at him, her brown eyes widening with concern. "How do you know? You said you weren't there."

"I was in my house, waiting to hear from him, when the feeling came to me that he was dead. That's why I drove to his place." Nate held her brown eyes with a steady gaze, daring her to question him.

She opened her mouth, but closed it again. He could see that she was uncomfortable with his answer, but not willing to argue and upset the tenuous truce and nascent understanding between them. They would have to go over the issue eventually, but it could wait.

"Okay," she said, flinching first, breaking eye contact and looking over his shoulder. "But if he didn't die until 1:26 Monday morning, why didn't he meet me at ten on Sunday night?"

"Around ten-thirty p.m., I got a text from him saying 'Don't come. You can't help. I don't want you blamed if something happens.' He knew something was wrong, but he wanted to handle it himself. Whatever it was must have been so big that he forgot about your meeting."

Loriana grinned, a wide, toothy smile. "I thought you always took Ingall's advice? He said not to come, and you didn't listen."

"And I ended up in trouble. Ingall was right, as usual." Nate smiled at Loriana. The space between them grew several degrees warmer, even if the sparks weren't visible to the naked eye.

"What were you planning on doing next?" she asked, pulling back and raising her voice to normal conversational levels.

"I was on my way to the quarantine camp in South Houston when you called. I wanted to see the place, talk to the staff, and meet some of the kids, especially the Tolokonsky children."

"I want to go with you. I want to help." She stretched one hand across the table, stopping short of grabbing Nate's hand by an inch.

"You don't need to do that. Besides, you have to go talk to the police." Nate looked at her small hand, ready to take his if he'd only move a little toward her. He wanted to move, but his head overruled his heart. The differences between them hadn't vanished. Fundamentally, they still weren't compatible. Maybe. Now wasn't the time for that discussion.

"How about if you come with me to the police, and we go to the camps together?" Her brown eyes pleaded with him and a small smile played on her soft lips.

"The detective in charge doesn't like me. Your credit with him will drop several points if I'm present." Nate tried to keep his expression serious, but it was hard not to soften when looking into those eyes. He smiled back at her.

"I'm innocent and so are you. I'd like you to be there with me. Please come," she said, knowing she had him won over and grinning back at him.

"Do you want to take two cars?" Nate surrendered to her as warning bells rang in his head and his heart leaped all at once.

"Can we leave mine somewhere?" she asked.

"We could leave it at my hotel. It's on the way to the police station."

"Okay." She took another drink from her glass, glancing at him over the top of the glass in a playful way. The word "hotel" had caught her attention, and with it an array of possible endings for the day came to mind.

When they finished lunch, Nate called Detective Janwari to let him know they were coming in to see him. The detective agreed to meet with Loriana, but suggested that Nate's presence was unnecessary. As they dropped Loriana's car off in the hotel parking lot, Nate tried not to think about what could happen when they came back to the hotel to get her car. His brain was miles ahead of all the things he still needed to do that day, leaping to visions of him inviting Loriana up to his room for a drink and to discuss what other opinions of hers might have changed. Alas, it was not to be.

∽

Tuesday, 1 p.m., Taylor High School.

JEANETTE PICCONE SAT in the high-school library at a round table with four other students. They ranged in age from fourteen to seventeen. Although she was the youngest, Jeanette was in charge. She was motivated, angry, and capable of organizing a detailed plan of action. She'd been raised in an atmosphere suffused with the memories of her murdered siblings. She wanted to exact vengeance in their memory. She wanted her parents to know that justice had finally been carried out. She wanted to bring them closure and end their suffering. She wanted the murderers to suffer and die as she imagined her siblings had died.

The trauma of death marked Jeanette's earliest memories and haunted her day-to-day life. One room of her home was a frozen shrine to the memory of her lost siblings, full of toys she could never touch and smiling pictures of her parents in happier days. Sometimes it seemed impossible that the pleasant, friendly people in those old pictures had anything to do with her grief-stricken, angry parents.

"Spread the word to everyone to be ready. I'm just waiting for one more piece of information, and then we go!" she said to the students gathered around her.

"I'll take care of it. Are you sure we have enough supplies?" asked Victor. He sat on her right side, anxiety on his face.

"Quit worrying," she said with irritation. "We've got four dozen pipe bombs and two hundred Molotov cocktails. People know to bring their own weapons. Once the wall between the parking lot and the basketball court is blown, we have to get in and out fast. The recreation area borders the living areas. We break out the windows, lob in the bottles, and get out."

"We've been over this," said Rig, the sixteen-year-old to her left, shrugging her off. His attention was wandering.

"We have to get this right!" said Jeanette. "Those creatures in that camp don't deserve to live. They've already killed countless numbers of people. If they get out of that facility, they could wipe out the whole city, maybe even the whole world. We must protect ourselves from them. Dad says that the doctors want those monsters to come out and live among us. They only have to touch bus seats, or ATM buttons, or grocery carts to wipe us all out. We can't let that happen!" A passionate flame burned in her eyes and her nostrils flared unattractively as she spoke.

The others around the table quickly agreed, hoping to stem the tide of yet another of Jeanette's diatribes. The bell rang signaling the end of the period. The teenagers collected binders, bags, cell phones, and tablets, and wended their ways through noisy, crowded halls, vanishing into the flow of unconcerned teenagers. Jeanette sometimes stared at the oblivious masses, amazed at their blindness to the danger surrounding them. She didn't understand how so many people could be uninterested in the matter of the Allergen Children.

Tuesday, 2 p.m., Houston Police Department.

DETECTIVE JANWARI WAS displeased by Nate's presence and suspicious of Loriana. He put Nate in an interview room by himself and took Loriana away to question her. Forty-five minutes later, the detective came back to Nate with questions that told Nate exactly what the detective was thinking.

"When did your relationship with Loriana Montilla end?"

"About six months ago."

"Why did it end?"

"Irreconcilable differences regarding religion and politics."

"How well did Father Ingall know Ms. Montilla?"

"They'd met."

"Was their relationship the reason yours ended?"

Nate stared at the detective trying to decide whether he was implying what Nate thought he was implying. "Are you asking whether Ingall had a relationship with Loriana? That's ridiculous. Ingall was committed to his vows and didn't have time to stray from them, even if he had wanted to. Ingall played a role in our breakup, but it was a philosophical role. He stood for everything I believe. He represented faith in humanity and in God. Loriana and I fought about religion and overall views of how we see the world. Ingall represented everything she didn't believe. Although, she told me today that some of her beliefs have changed."

"Are you aware that Ms. Montilla was in contact with Father Ingall recently?"

"Loriana told me today that she was supposed to meet with Ingall the night he died, regarding his work on behalf of the Allergen Children."

"Were you bothered by the fact that they were meeting?"

"If I'd known about it, no, I wouldn't have been bothered. I would have been surprised because, until today, I would have sworn Loriana had no interest in Ingall's work. She used to think his work was pointless and dangerous."

"Ms. Montilla works for a senator who has been vocal in his public safety stance against the Allergen Children. Do you think she could have killed your brother, either to support the senator's work or because she felt Father Ingall's work was endangering the public?"

"No! I don't think Loriana had anything to do with Ingall's death."

The detective's eyes bored into Nate's head. Nate could see that Janwari liked the idea of a love triangle. At the same time, the detective was suspicious of Loriana's motives in going to see Ingall. A check of computer and phone records would show that Nate hadn't been in contact with Loriana for months. Ingall's records and Loriana's would show the same, with the exception of the call to set up their meeting. The love-triangle idea would be eliminated fairly quickly, but Loriana would still be on Detective Janwari's radar as a suspect. Nate had never asked Loriana what she had done after Ingall had failed to meet her. He hoped she'd gone somewhere with security cameras, so she would have an alibi for the time of Ingall's death.

"Do you know where Ms. Montilla was at the time of Father Ingall's death?" asked the detective. Nate wondered if the man could see his thoughts flowing across his face.

"No. I didn't ask her."

"Why not?"

"Because I don't think she was involved in his death."

The detective was still studying Nate, waiting for him to assimilate the suggestion. The detective thought Nate was too in love with his ex-girlfriend to see that she might have killed his brother. A seed of doubt formed in Nate's mind. Nate should have asked Loriana where she had been. He only had her word that she'd changed her mind on the Allergen Children. She could have made up the whole change of heart to cover her real purpose. He had no proof that she carried the mutation. He had taken everything she had said as truth because he was still in love with her and wanted to believe she'd changed. Then again, why would she come to talk to him if she hadn't changed her mind? She could have gone back to Austin without contacting him.

"When will you release my brother's body for burial?" Nate asked, changing the subject.

"In cases like this, a full autopsy has to be completed, but it should only take a few days. The medical examiner will call you." A smug smile spread across the detective's face. "You are free to go, Mr. Bryan. We'll contact you if we have any more questions," said the detective.

"Is Ms. Montilla free to go as well?"

"She is."

Nate found Loriana waiting for him in the lobby, checking her email on her phone.

"They think you killed Ingall," he said.

"I know." She didn't look up from her phone.

"They'll be looking into where you were when he died."

"I know."

She was still reading an email, not meeting his eyes.

"Where were you?" he asked.

"Do you really think I killed Ingall?" Her eyes came up at last, cloudy, angry, and sad. Her gravelly voice cracked a bit.

"No. I want to know if you have an alibi. The less time the police spend on you, the sooner they can get back to finding Ingall's murderer." Nate tried to sound like he meant what he said, like he was unhappy with the police for suspecting her.

She gave him an evaluating look before shrugging. "I was tired. I waited outside his office building until eleven-thirty. If there are cameras around his building, they should confirm that. Then I gave up and drove to my sister's house. I got there after midnight. Mari was waiting up for me because I called to tell her I was coming into town and needed a place to sleep. We talked for about forty-five minutes, and then she went to bed. I did some email until around 1:45, then went to bed. My sister lives in Spring."

If the police could confirm Loriana's arrival time at her sister's house and her computer activity, she wouldn't be a suspect. Spring, north of Houston, was a solid hour's drive from Ingall's residence building. If she was telling Nate the truth . . .

"Do you still want to go with me to the camp?" he asked, trying to keep his voice even. He could still feel that spark of warmth that had shot between them at lunchtime, but the logical voice in his head wanted to see how she fared in the camp. If she had told him the truth, if she really did have the mutation, she would have nothing to fear in the camps and no need to take the precautions he would have to take when interacting with the children.

"Yes," she said.

"Let's go," he said, turning toward the building's exit.

CHAPTER 5

Tuesday, 4 p.m., Camp Lambda.

At first glance, Camp Lambda, in South Houston, looked like any large, nondescript business complex. On second glance, the obvious security features gave it the feel of a federal courthouse or detention center. Large concrete blocks surrounded the building's exterior walls. They'd been installed to fend off vehicular attack, with little thought given to aesthetics. The parking lot was walled in by a hedge, and an armed guard was stationed in a hut at the entrance. Cameras covered every angle in the parking lot and around the facility.

After getting clearance to park, Nate and Loriana walked toward the building's main entrance. Sounds of children playing emanated from behind a sixteen-foot-tall concrete wall topped with razor wire. The sounds of a ball bouncing on a court and the accompanying calls to pass the ball told Nate a basketball game was in progress somewhere over the wall. Nate and Loriana reached the main doors, which didn't slide open immediately as expected. Instead, they had to ring a bell, identify themselves over an intercom system, and be buzzed in after acknowledging directions to proceed immediately to the front desk. The tight security was glaringly incongruent with the children's laughter.

A young receptionist greeted them. "Please have a seat. Dr. Archepane and Ms. Jemington have been informed of your arrival, but safety protocols have to be followed before they can meet you. They've been on the children's side of the building." She smiled warmly. Nate thought she looked about the age of his undergraduate students.

Nate got the impression that the young woman thought he knew the ins and outs of life in the camps and would understand the delay. Her tone acknowledged him as an insider, someone trusted. Nate didn't feel he deserved her confidence, but was glad of the welcome. Nate and Loriana sat in a small grouping of institutional plastic chairs in the small lobby.

As they waited, the receptionist offered her condolences on Ingall's death. She came out from behind her desk as if she wanted to talk, but was called away by her ringing phone before she could say anything more.

Twenty minutes later, Loriana and Nate were greeted simultaneously from two directions. Swiveling his head to look at both quickly, Nate saw a makeup-free, middle-aged woman in a business jacket and skirt and a white-haired man in khaki slacks with a stethoscope around his neck; both had wet hair. Their first words were jumbled offers of condolences.

The doctor asserted himself, talking loudly over the woman, who dropped into silence. "Mr. Bryan, I'm Dr. Stellan Archepane. We will miss your brother. Father Ingall was a godsend to us here. He was a wonderful advocate and guide for the older children. I don't know how we'll ever replace him." He reached out and shook hands with Nate vigorously.

"Thank you, Sir," Nate replied, turning to Loriana. "This is a friend of mine, Loriana Montilla. Mr. Tolokonsky must have called to let you know I was coming. Thank you for seeing me."

The middle-aged woman said, "We appreciate your interest in the facility and the children. I'm Hannah Jemington, the executive administrator here at Camp Lambda. Mr. Tolokonsky said you had questions and that you were interested in helping us. Will you be taking over some of your brother's work?"

"I've always been a supporter of Ingall's work with the children. I don't have his background and training and can't envision that I could ever replace him in working directly with the children, but I do plan to help promote the children's cause."

"Do the police have any idea who killed Father Ingall?" asked Ms. Jemington.

"Not as far as I know. Have the police been here to ask questions yet?" asked Nate.

"The police *here*?" replied Dr. Archepane. "They called and spoke to several of us, but I doubt any of them will come out here. Most people are afraid to even enter the building. They're afraid that breathing the same air as the children might kill them." He shook his mane of damp white hair and crossed his arms on his chest, disdain on his face. "Come into my office and sit down," he said, turning to lead them all down a sterile, white corridor to an office with his name on the door.

The small office was sparsely furnished and looked to be used only for formal meetings. The only personal items in the office were the diplomas on the wall confirming the doctor's various certifications. Dr. Archepane apparently didn't spend much time seated behind his desk.

Once they were arrayed around the bare desk, Ms. Jemington picked up the conversation. "Father Ingall was one of the few nonfamily visitors we get here. Most of the staff and teachers are carriers of the mutation and, therefore, are immune to its effects. We've had a few doctors and nurses rotate through in training who weren't carriers, but, otherwise, noncarriers avoid coming here," said Ms. Jemington.

"Do you know if Father Ingall had received any more threats than usual or had any personal problems lately?" Nate began. "Did he seem worried or bothered by anything? I'd really like to know what happened to him. If the police can't be bothered to come speak to his colleagues here at the facility, I have to wonder what kind of an investigation they are running."

Ms. Jemington and Dr. Archepane both started to speak at once, but, again, the doctor won out. "Father Ingall was very much himself when he was here the other night. He brought some items for the children and stayed to talk to them about the progress the researchers have been making. He seemed excited that Dr. Park's plan could really work. If anything, he seemed optimistic about the future, looking forward to positive changes in the area of the children's rights."

"We talked about the day the children re-enter society and what precautions they'll have to take," said Ms. Jemington.

"Could the children rejoin society now?" Nate asked.

"Absolutely," said the white-haired doctor, with a vigorous nod. "With simple precautions, the teenagers would have no problems re-entering society right now. The older ones with an understanding of their condition are quite mindful of the danger they pose to other people. When you meet them, don't be surprised if they seem standoffish. It took Father Ingall months to break down that barrier and let them know he wasn't afraid of them."

"What about the younger children? You don't think they can be released yet?" asked Loriana, a curious expression on her face.

"No. They lack the understanding of their condition and its dangers. Until they reach an age of appropriate caution, they require a certain degree of isolation from the general public," said the doctor, with a confirming nod from Ms. Jemington.

"What's your opinion of the research? The idea that the population as a whole should be treated to become more like the children here—do you think it will work?" asked Nate.

"I've reviewed the studies, and the research is sound. A large number of immunological pathologies could be alleviated or even eradicated by treating the entire population with a vaccination that would induce a condition like what the children carry. Most cancer could completely disappear. Whether the public as a whole or our lawmakers will see it that way, I can't say. They might be distrustful of being made to excrete a deadly substance. Ingrained fear of the condition will have to be overcome. We were looking forward to Father Ingall leading the way in that battle. Now I don't know who will be as trusted a voice to the people. Mr. Tolokonsky is willing, but he lacks the diplomatic skills, and he is seen as biased by his connections to the issue," said Dr. Archepane.

"Mr. Tolokonsky mentioned a number of recent changes here in terms of security: restrictions to freedom of movement for the children, monitoring of activities. What's your opinion of these changes?" Nate asked.

The doctor and the administrator exchanged a cautious glance. He let her answer this time. "We are worried about the changes. The children aren't blind to what is happening. This is their home. Changes stand out here as much as if you rearranged the furniture in your own house and repainted the walls. The new restrictions scare them. A few of our teenagers are inclined to rebel at any curtailment of what little freedom they have. To place further restrictions on them could be disastrous for the proper functioning of this facility."

"In what way?"

Again, glances flew between the doctor and his coworker. "They'll start with nonviolent civil disobedience of the rules and programs," said the doctor. "From there, if no one responds to their concerns, I wouldn't be surprised if some of the older children tried to escape. The children are aware of the media reports and bills being discussed. They are terrified that they might be forcibly sterilized, held in containment for life, or even killed. They fear the facility will be attacked. Some of them were caught organizing an armed resistance, but Father Ingall explained that arming themselves would only make the public fear them more. He was a gifted counselor. Things may deteriorate around here without him, especially since some of the children have relatives who favor even more radical action."

"The tension in the atmosphere here has doubled since we learned of Father Ingall's death. He was well-liked, trusted, respected. The children knew he would never let anything happen to them. They feel bereft and exposed without him," said Ms. Jemington. "Some of the teenagers see his death as a personal attack on them. They expect people to come for them at any moment."

Loriana sat forward in her chair, "In such a charged atmosphere, what would happen if a lawmaker suggested moving all the children to a high-security prison in West Texas, away from any major population centers?"

A look of horror passed over the doctor's face. "Please tell me that isn't going to happen."

"The teenagers and their families would go to war," said Ms. Jemington. "If someone tried to move the children away from their families, I don't think we would be able to stop the children from resisting by any means at their disposal. The children are quite resourceful. If they don't escape and go into hiding, they would try to defend themselves here. It would end with some sort of armed standoff, followed by a SWAT raid and a lot of deaths."

"The children know they can't win against the government if it comes to that, but they don't care," said Dr. Archepane. "They've taken the motto 'Live free or die,' which won out in a close vote over 'Give me liberty or give me death.'" The doctor gave a sad smile when Nate raised his eyebrows at him. "The children have had year-round education since entering the facility. Most of the teenagers have completed high-school-level work and have begun online college course work. The oldest already have university degrees. The Tolokonskys' oldest boy has a bachelor's degree in history and is working on one in chemistry. They are intelligent and well informed. I don't encourage the revolutionary spirit here, but I'd have to be blind not to be aware of it."

"In short, unless the tide turns in the children's favor, this place is going to explode," Nate said.

"Father Ingall's death may have helped light the fuse," said Dr. Archepane. "His efforts and his calming presence were the only things holding everyone in check."

"Can I speak to the Tolokonsky children?" Nate asked.

"Yes, of course. They are expecting you. They should be finishing dinner and heading into their evening free time. Many family members arrive in the evening for visits," said Ms. Jemington with a glance at the time. "We can provide you with gloves, and you are required to cover any exposed skin below the neck." Her eyes flicked over Loriana's bare arms and décolletage. "Do you have a change of clothing with you? If not, we can give you coveralls, but the children don't like them. The coveralls look like biohazard suits, which the teenagers find a bit insulting."

"I have extra clothing with me, but Loriana doesn't." Nate pointed to a backpack he'd carried in with him.

"It doesn't matter," Loriana said. "I'm a carrier, so the secretions can't hurt me. I don't want to insult the kids. Could I wear these clothes in to see them and borrow something to change into when I come out? I'll bring it back when I come to get my own clothes. You will keep our clothes for decontamination, right?"

"Yes, that's fine," said the doctor with relief in his eyes. "Anything we can do to avoid upsetting the children's sensibilities would be best."

Nate smiled at Loriana, relieved by the fact that she hadn't lied about being a carrier.

Ms. Jemington handed Nate a deceptively thin pair of gloves and made a call to have his backpack waiting for him in the decontamination area. The group walked through a series of corridors and security doors, past medical and administrative areas to a large lounge area. The room was comfortably furnished with deep couches and chairs, lots of tables for working or studying, and soft throw rugs underfoot. It looked like a dorm lounge or an oversized living room. The feel of the building changed in the lounge and, with it, so did Ms. Jemington's attitude. Instead of behaving as a cool business administrator, she moved into the room greeting students and smiling beneficently down on her charges like the beloved principal or head mistress of a boarding school.

About twenty teenagers had draped themselves around the room, some with legs in intertwined piles, others leaning against each other. Most had earbuds in their ears and tablet computers in their hands. Almost all of their heads came up and scrutinized Loriana and Nate as they entered the room in Ms. Jemington's wake. Nate saw a few startled looks of recognition, which told him that what little resemblance he had to Ingall was noticed. Eyes darted around the room, meeting in silent consultation before returning to focus on the newcomers. Four of the oldest students removed their earbuds and stood up.

A tall, blonde, young man held out his hand to shake Nate's and said, "Mr. Bryan? I'm Oleksandr Tolokonsky. We heard about your brother. We are really sorry for your loss. We'll miss him, too."

Oleksandr looked like a younger version of his father, blond and blue-eyed with the physique of an athlete, complete with thick neck and bulging biceps. Nate shook his hand without hesitation, entirely forgetting that without gloves he'd have gone into anaphylactic shock and died. In his eyes, they were kids grieving the same loss that he was.

As they shook hands, the tension in the room eased, as if the teens had all started breathing again.

A pale-skinned girl with a delicate, pixie face stepped forward. "I am Anya Tolokonsky. Pleased to meet you, Sir," she said as she shook hands. She was tall with narrow hips and long legs, as lean as a fashion model, wearing skintight jeans and a loose, layered tank top that fluttered around her waist as she moved. Nate thought she looked like a more mature version of her younger sister, Elizaveta.

Another teenager, maybe seventeen or eighteen years old, stepped forward. He was as dark of complexion as the Tolokonskys were light. "I'm Sam Nganadomi. Thanks for coming here."

A third young man, looking older than the rest, his face shadowed with a dark beard that he had shaved closely, advanced next. "I'm Omar Yassine. We hope they catch whoever killed Father Ingall."

Glancing beyond the four tall, young people around him, Nate saw that the other children had remained in their positions, waiting and watching. They all looked to be younger than the four before him, maybe thirteen to fifteen years old.

"Come sit down," said Omar, directing Nate and Loriana toward a corner of the room furnished with a sofa and three overstuffed chairs.

Loriana and Nate sat on the sofa. The three boys took the overstuffed chairs. Anya perched on the arm of her brother's chair, a habitual crease between her blue eyes from anxiety or concern.

Oleksandr glanced at Omar before speaking, got a nod to go ahead, and said, "Do the police have any idea who killed Father Ingall?"

"I don't know. If they do, they haven't told me anything about it."

A variety of derisive snorts and huffing breaths were released. "You'd think they'd start with the most obvious suspect, that asshole Piccone," said Sam. "He'd do anything to keep us all locked up for the rest of our lives. Look at what he's doing to Omar."

"What's he doing to Omar?" Loriana asked, looking at the serious young man with the five o'clock shadow on his face.

"He's trying to get me transferred out of here to an adult prison. He says that since I'm nineteen and legally an adult, I shouldn't be kept here with the others. He wants us all transferred to higher-security prisons as we age out of the school here."

"Surely, no one would agree to that. You haven't committed any crime! Besides, the prisons wouldn't want you, since they'd have to isolate you away from the other prisoners," said Loriana.

"As far as Piccone is concerned, I committed a crime by being born! He'd be happy to see me in solitary confinement the rest of my life." Omar's tone was gentle but condescending as he explained basic facts to his apparently naïve listeners.

Nate asked, "Aside from Piccone, was there anyone or anything else troubling him? You all saw him the day before he died, right? How did he seem to you? Was he the same as ever? Worried? Distracted? Did he do anything differently?"

Anya said, "He was the same as ever. If anything, he was more positive. He was excited about Dr. Park's idea to vaccinate everyone so that we could be around them. He told us all the details of the study trial being planned—how he was going to be the first one vaccinated. He said he couldn't wait to come here and give us all hugs and handshakes without gloves." A tear fell down her cheek, but she brushed it away. "They killed him to slow down the trial. To keep us locked up forever."

"That's not going to happen! We won't let it," said Omar.

"The trial will go on, even without Ingall," Nate said.

"It could take years to convince people that the vaccination will be good for them. Look at how long it takes to implement new vaccines against known diseases. People are afraid of the shot more than the disease. The medical community will have to convince everyone to get a shot to give them a condition that they're afraid of. That's not going to be easy," said Oleksandr.

"But in the meantime, as more people get vaccinated and you use simple precautions to prevent deaths, people will see that you can be released to live your lives. As the numbers of vaccinated people rise, keeping you in isolation or quarantine will become pointless. They'll have to release you," Nate said.

"That's what Father Ingall said last week," said Anya. "And then he was murdered."

Silence fell. The whole room went still.

"Some of us can't wait years. We may get chucked into regular prisons or ordered to be sterilized before that happens. The populace will either sit on the fence, too afraid to take a position, or sit back and enjoy the schadenfreude, just happy to see someone else getting screwed over as long as it isn't them," said Omar.

"Damn straight!" said Sam, as the others nodded.

"We'll be gone before it comes to that," said Oleksandr.

Anya thumped his arm with a closed fist, and Omar frowned him down.

"What!? If my father sent him to talk to us, it's okay to talk!" said Oleksandr.

"Don't worry about us," Nate said. "We're on your side."

"Absolutely!" said Loriana, giving the boy a knowing wink.

Nate said, "A breakout would definitely be a smarter move than an open battle. By vanishing into the population and being careful not to kill anyone accidentally, you'd win much more support in the long run. However, I wouldn't rush into that either. Being on the run is dangerous. Here, you have the support of your families and doctors, access to good food and shelter, and information. By going into hiding, you'd be cut off from all contact with your families and anyone who could help you in an emergency. Everyone you know would be monitored by authorities who are on the lookout for you. Things aren't as desperate as that yet."

A smile spread across Omar's face. "You sound like Father Ingall. He made us promise to wait and see how the public reacts to the vaccination idea." The smile vanished, and the dark, serious look returned to his face. "We agreed to wait, but if anything holds up the vaccination trials, all bets are off. Father Ingall is dead. He was the only one who could convince everyone that getting the vaccination is the best course."

"He wasn't the only one!" said Loriana. "Lots of others are fighting for you, too!"

"Maybe so," said Sam. "But we don't have much faith in people who claim to be on our side and yet are afraid of us. Father Ingall wasn't afraid of us. Everyone else who has come here talked about our situation as if we were a philosophical exercise, an interesting thought problem, or a challenging research project. They don't see us as thinking, breathing individuals. They are afraid to shake our hands."

"I'm not," Nate said.

Omar gave him an appraising look. "You're good, but you're not Father Ingall. You don't have his air of honesty or that ability to instantly connect with people and make them want to trust you and follow your lead."

Nate's respect for Omar's intelligence ratcheted up several notches. "No, I don't have Ingall's gifts. We won't be able to replace him with any single person. But several people working together could do it."

Silence fell again, this time allowing the tension in the conversation to fade.

"If Dad can organize it, we're coming to the funeral," said Anya, changing the subject.

"We want to pay our respects, but we also think it's time we got in front of some news cameras," said Omar. "We need people to see that we are just like them, not inhuman monsters. It's easier to demonize us if we don't have our faces in the public view. We need to make people see us and not fear us. Taking our rights and imprisoning us will seem wrong to more people if they can put a face to our names."

"I agree. I hope to see you there. The funeral hasn't been scheduled yet, but I'll let Mr. Tolokonsky know when it is. If anyone can find a way to get you there, he can," Nate said.

Nate glanced around. The lounge was filling with families, and the volume of conversation had risen. He turned the conversation to more general topics, asking the teenagers about their fields of study and how they spent their days in order to get a better picture of life in the camps. From the responses he got, Nate could tell that the new restrictions on movement and the monitoring of activities and information rankled. Other families and children approached Nate and Loriana, offering condolences.

After a while, Ms. Jemington rejoined them. "Visiting hours are almost over. Only family members who are staying the night at the camp are allowed to remain inside visiting areas after seven o'clock. Those who are leaving need to begin out-processing procedures in order to be out of the building by the time the doors lock at eight-thirty."

Loriana and Nate stood up. "I will be working on your side. I'll even volunteer for the vaccine trial," Nate said to the four earnest teens gathered around him to say their goodbyes. "I know it's asking a lot, given how long this has taken, but please don't do anything drastic. Good people are doing everything they can to help you. Humanity as a whole can choose to do the right thing, though sometimes they need a nudge in the right direction."

"Good night, Mr. Bryan. It was nice to meet you," said Anya.

They shook hands and followed Ms. Jemington out of the room. Loriana and Nate were directed to decontamination showers, provided with robes, and had their clothes taken away in labeled plastic bags. Nate finished first and changed into his spare clothes, which he found waiting for him. He waited for Loriana in the lobby, checking his messages on his phone. She emerged ten minutes later from the women's side of the decontamination area, just as Ms. Jemington had earlier in the day. Her long brown hair hung damply on her shoulders, and her face was bare of makeup. She wore medical scrubs that were too large. She'd rolled the pants at the ankles. The shirt came down well over her hips, swallowing her upper body like a tent. On her feet, instead of her usual stylish heels, she wore disposable flip-flops. Nate chuckled a little when he saw her.

"Thanks," she said, crinkling her slightly crooked nose. "I look ridiculous."

"You look marvelous. Thanks for doing this. The kids wouldn't have been so talkative if you'd come in to see them in a biohazard suit. We won their confidence." He gave her a smile and was rewarded with a warm look in her brown eyes.

"*You* won their confidence," she said. "I didn't do anything. Now, how are we going to help them? You want to solve Ingall's murder first, don't you? Do you intend to carry through on that promise you made to be part of the trial? That might interfere with your teaching." Her face showed both skepticism at the wisdom of his decision and amazement at his generosity.

"I need to do this. Maybe exposing whoever killed Ingall will help motivate people to support the children. I'll start with solving Ingall's murder. I'm not worried about the teaching. If I'm still teaching after the trials, think of all the students I can talk to about getting the treatment."

"You are a good man, Nate." Loriana stood on her toes and kissed him on the cheek and give him a look of admiration. "I was an idiot."

Nate ignored the warnings in his head about their incompatibility and grabbed her around the waist, collapsing her tent of a shirt. He kissed her soft lips, which had turned automatically up to his. Mindful of the time, he let her go quickly, hoping that they could continue later.

His hopes were dashed as they pulled into the hotel parking lot. A fire engine blocked half the lot, forcing them to go to an alternate entrance on the opposite side of the hotel from where they'd left Loriana's car. Walking around, they found the firefighters in clean-up mode, rolling hoses and preparing to leave. Nate quickly spotted the reason for the firefighters' presence in the lot: the charred and smoking remains of a car. As Loriana gasped at the sight before them, Nate realized the car was Loriana's.

She ran forward to the nearest police officer, who stood talking to a Houston Fire Department lieutenant.

"What happened to my car?" she asked, her voice pitched higher than usual with fear.

"This was your car, Ma'am?" asked the police officer.

"Yes, we left it here earlier this evening," she said.

"Are you staying here at the hotel?" asked the officer.

"No, my friend is staying here. We needed to go somewhere this evening and thought it would be easier to take only one car. We left mine here and took his. How did my car catch fire?" Loriana's eyes wandered back to the charred, smoking remains of her car, a look of shocked horror on her face.

The firefighter said, "Someone stuck a rag in a gas can, placed it under the car, lit the rag, and left it to burn." He looked curiously at Loriana's clothing. Then the fireman said goodbye to the police officer and stepped back to his engine, where the task of packing up the hoses had begun.

As the police officer took down Loriana's name and address, she shivered in the night air. Although it was nine at night, heat still radiated off the concrete roads and asphalt parking lots around them. However, Loriana was only wearing oversized scrubs, her hair was still damp, and she'd had a shock. A light breeze unsettled the air around them. Nate offered to get her a jacket from his room and left to fetch it.

Unlocking the door with his card key, Nate hustled into the room intent on getting the windbreaker he'd left on the desk for Loriana. Consequently, he didn't notice that something wasn't right until he'd passed the microwave and coffee area at the front of the room and was standing by the bed.

CHAPTER 6

Tuesday, 9 p.m., hotel.

Someone had searched the room. All the drawers were open. The closet was open. Nate's jacket was on the floor. A wave of adrenalin pulsed through him, and he braced himself, expecting an attack, but none came. Whoever had been in the room was gone. Whatever they'd been looking for, they couldn't have found it. He didn't have anything of any value. Stepping out into the hall again, Nate considered what to do next. Searching his room and burning Loriana's car could have been a way to tell them to stop looking into Ingall's death. Perhaps he was being warned to back off. Then again, maybe someone really did want something. He didn't have anything anyone would want. However, Loriana might. She'd said that she had no evidence against Senator Coalember, but what if she did? What if she had been the target tonight instead of him?

Nate pulled his phone out and called Detective Janwari. Everything had to be connected to Ingall's death.

The detective answered, and Nate explained what had happened. Janwari asked Nate to stay at the hotel and said that he would be there shortly. Nate took the jacket back down to Loriana and let the police officers know that another crime scene awaited them inside.

Nate and Loriana spent the next five hours at the police station. In the wee hours of the morning, Loriana's sister picked her up, taking Loriana to her house for what remained of the night. Nate returned to the hotel, where he was given another room, with apologies from the management. The manager on duty couldn't express how sorry he was that such an incident had occurred while Nate was a guest at his establishment. Nate accepted the man's apologies as quickly as he could, hung the "Do Not Disturb" sign, and fell into bed in a room identical to the one he'd been in before, only two floors up.

Five hours later he awoke, groggily, to the sound of his phone ringing.

"Hello?"

"Mr. Bryan? This is Vera Tolokonsky."

Nate sat up hastily, eyes still unfocused, and tried to gather his wits back from the depths of whatever dream he'd been having. "Mrs. Tolokonsky, hello. What can I do for you?"

"I wanted to tell you that if anyone at the camp suggested that Father Ingall was involved in any sort of inappropriate relationship, don't believe it. He was a wonderful, intelligent man—kind, caring, and decent. All of which made him extremely attractive, especially to a teenager engulfed by her first crush. But Father Ingall did everything as he should."

"I see. Your daughter fell in love with him?"

"Yes. She'd begun requesting additional counseling sessions so that she could spend more time with him. I think some of the staff at the camp might have noticed her attachment to him, too. But if anyone says that he did anything he shouldn't have, please ignore them."

"Thank you for telling me. I'd gotten hints that something of that nature had happened. It wasn't the first time. Ingall had had that happen when he had worked as a psychologist as well. He was trained to handle it." Nate suppressed a laugh. Ingall had always underrated himself with women. He'd once asked Nate why any woman would be attracted to an underweight scarecrow of a man with only tufts of brown hair left on top of his head (since most of it had migrated down around his ears and the back of his head). Of course, the answer had been simple: To some people, character was everything, and Ingall had had that by the bucketful. His exterior may not have been movie-star quality, but his soul had been vibrantly beautiful. Although, in his humility, Ingall had always underrated his own character, too.

"I'm so glad you understand. I hope the police don't hear about it. They'll twist it into something it wasn't," said Vera Tolokonsky.

"No one at the camp mentioned it to me. They didn't think the police would bother to go out there to talk to them. They think the police are too afraid of contact with the children to enter the building."

"That is probably true." She sighed in recognition of the failings of the world and its systems.

Another thought occurred to Nate, so he decided to test her response to it. "Mrs. Tolokonsky, I wanted to speak to you regarding your other daughter."

"Elizaveta? What about her?"

"I noticed while I was at your house that she had bruises on her arm and black paint on her fingers. Driving in town, I saw graffiti in support of the children scrawled along the freeway. Obviously, it's a huge leap to connect that to your daughter. However, if she was spray painting slogans on underpasses, bridges, and walls, I would be worried about her safety. Some of the places were dangerous to reach."

Silence met his statement. He wondered whether she knew about the activities and supported them or if he had shocked her.

"Mr. Bryan, until you mentioned it, I would not have thought my daughter had the time or opportunity to paint graffiti on roadways, but I will look into the matter. She is much too young to be out doing such things."

It struck him that her daughter's age was the only part of the activity that Mrs. Tolokonsky took issue with. Did that mean that, if Elizaveta were older, Mrs. Tolokonsky wouldn't mind her daughter risking arrest and her life in dangerous places?

"She would need someone to drive her. Does she have older friends willing to help her?" asked Nate.

"Yes, within our community, those who are working for the release of their siblings, as she is. Many of us have children who are carriers. The young adults and teenagers want to help get their siblings released. Some of them might have decided to spread the word with graffiti."

"Anyone in particular that you can think of?" Nate wasn't sure why he was asking. It was none of his business.

"The younger brother of a friend of Oleksandr's. Did you meet Omar in the camp?"

"Yes. He's an intelligent young man."

"Omar is very smart. His younger brother, Karim, however, is a thoughtless hothead."

"Perhaps age will bring wisdom. Teenagers aren't known for thinking through the consequences of their actions."

"That depends on the teenager," she said, "and the influences upon him . . ."

Nate could hear that she had more to say, something that she was turning over in her mind. He muttered a sound of agreement. "What sort of influences?"

She paused, looking for the right words. "One or two of the families advocate more extreme action than my husband and I are willing to take."

"How extreme?"

"They believe that it is the natural order for those without the mutation to die out. They consider hastening that event an acceptable policy. The majority in our community disagree with such ideas. Most of us have relatives who aren't carriers of the mutations. We don't want to see innocent people injured."

Nate's mind whirled. He didn't know how to respond, so he veered away from the violence he was envisioning and back to a safer subject. "You and your husband may want to examine the influences on Elizaveta."

"Yes," she said without rancor, almost tonelessly.

"Other than the philosophical disagreements he had with your husband, did Ingall have differences of opinion with any of the others in your community? Perhaps with those who hold more radical opinions on how to proceed?"

"Father Ingall was loved and respected. I can't imagine anyone in our group would hurt him."

"Not even if they believed he should die according to the natural order?"

"Not even then. Anyone targeting Father Ingall would be alienated from the community. Besides, everyone knew that we desperately needed his help."

"I understand. Thank you for calling me, Mrs. Tolokonsky."

"You are welcome. I look forward to seeing more of you. Oleksandr told me that you were volunteering for the trials."

"Yes. It's the right thing to do."

"Many people wouldn't see it that way," she said.

"Not yet, but we will convince them." Nate tried to sound positive. They both envisioned the obstacles and battles still to come.

The conversation ended, and Nate tumbled back down onto his pillow, wondering if he would ever go back to San Marcos. Ingall's life was replacing his in his head in more ways than he had thought possible. Nate wasn't sure that Ingall would have approved of that. Nate liked teaching, but it was never a matter of life or death, or of freedom or imprisonment. The life-or-death nature of pharmaceutical work had been what had driven him out of medical research. The more he learned about the forces surrounding Ingall's murder, the more he felt out of his depth, overwhelmed. Perhaps he wasn't meant for research anymore. Perhaps he was meant to go back to teaching and convince students to get treated by discussing the biochemistry of the trials with them.

Nate wished he could ask Ingall to advise him on what to do next. Then, the knowledge that Ingall was truly gone chilled him as if a bucket of ice water had been poured over his head. Nate gasped hard, forcing himself to breathe, before flinging himself into the shower, shaking with grief.

Nate stood and let the water run over his back, his head leaning against the cold white tiles. The words that came to him were Ingall's, speaking at their parents' funeral. Ingall had spoken of their parents' souls, forever together, rejoining their loved ones who had gone before them. He had talked about his absolute knowledge that he would meet his parents again someday when it was his time. Nate struggled with eternity, with God, and with souls. Ingall's arguments had convinced him that faith could coexist with science, that faith wasn't a foolish dream but a powerful tool in life.

At other low points in his life, most recently when he'd broken up with Loriana, Ingall's advice had brought him warmth and helped him remember that things would get better. Today, remembering Ingall's words wasn't helping. When Nate emerged from the shower, cold and hollow inside, all he could see was that he was alone, under attack, and failing miserably at what he had set out to do. The problems felt too overwhelming to contemplate, but he forced himself to look at the options. The likelihood of someone within the children's community killing Ingall seemed remote. Ingall had almost no private life, so a personal motive was unlikely. That left the whole group of people who feared and hated the children. He needed to consider whoever had torched the car and searched the room, too. He'd have to talk to Loriana about that.

Lying on the bed a moment later, barefooted and in jeans and a t-shirt, Nate decided the hollow feeling was most likely hunger. Hunger was something he could handle. He picked up his phone and searched for nearby breakfast restaurants, somewhere that served sausage and eggs—filling, protein-based food, not just pastries and coffee. Being tired and hungry had serious consequences for his state of mind.

Over an omelet containing ham, cheese, onion, and bell pepper, with a side of buttered toast, Nate decided to focus on what to say to Loriana. Her car hadn't been burned and his room searched for no reason. Someone was looking for something. He didn't have anything, so it stood to reason that she did, or that they thought she did. As he finished eating, his phone rang, and he decided the best approach was the direct one.

"Hello," Nate said.

"Nate? It's me. Are you okay?" responded Loriana's low voice.

"I'm fine. Why wouldn't I be?"

"Last night left me a little on edge." She hesitated, drawing in a deep breath.

"Loriana, why would someone search my room and burn your car? I don't have anything that anyone might want. The only reason someone would search my room is if they thought you had given me something. What do you think that might be?"

She inhaled sharply, her husky voice trembling a little as she said, "I don't . . . I'm not sure. Look, Nate, I don't want to talk about this on the phone. Can we meet?"

Disappointment filled him. She was hiding something. "Where and when?" Nate asked, his tone flat and impersonal.

"I don't know. Somewhere private, not out in public."

"How about a church?"

"A church?"

"Yeah. A church." Nate didn't add that maybe being near a house of God would encourage truthfulness on her part. She might counter that she didn't believe in God, which he didn't want to hear. Plus, Nate didn't need to antagonize her. She might change her mind about telling him the truth.

"What church?"

"Let me look one up, and I'll text you the address. What time is good for you?"

"Two p.m.?"

"Okay." Nate finished breakfast, used his phone to find a church nearby, texted the address to Loriana, paid the bill, and returned to the hotel with time to fill before meeting her.

Standing in the middle of the lobby, he felt the urge come over him to do something more productive than sleep until it was time to meet Loriana. Ingall's main nemesis remained on the list of people to contact. Nate pulled out his phone and left a message for Landon Piccone to call him regarding Ingall's death. He included the fact that he wasn't a reporter looking for a quote, but was Ingall's brother. Nate didn't know whether Piccone would call him back, but it was worth a shot.

Hopping in his car, Nate ended up almost involuntarily outside Ingall's offices. Deacon Matthias might be willing to confirm Mrs. Tolokonsky's story about her daughter falling for Ingall, since Nate already had the basics of it. Plus, he wouldn't have heard about the plot to move the kids to West Texas. Not to mention, Nate needed to see what had to be done about Ingall's funeral.

❧

Wednesday, 10 a.m., Ingall's offices.

"NATE, HOW ARE you?" said Matthias when Nate found him at his desk.

"All right. I found out that Ingall was supposed to meet my former fiancée, Loriana, the night he died, but he never showed up for the meeting. She was coming to tell him that she'd stumbled across a plan to have all of the children moved from the small facilities in their hometowns to one large prison facility out in West Texas. The senator she works for received very generous donations from the company intent on building the facility. The senator was going to present the whole thing as a matter of public safety, recommending the children be moved away from population centers."

"But they can't!" said Matthias, horrified shock filling his eyes.

"We're hoping he won't. The Tolokonskys got wind of the scheme and threatened to bring the issue of bribery to light if the senator proposes moving the children."

"Oh! Thank goodness!"

"Well, it's a little more complicated than that. Tolokonsky may be blackmailing the senator for support on key votes regarding the children."

"Oh! I see." He closed his eyes, put one hand over his mouth, and slumped his head forward over his desk. When he looked up, a pained expression filled his eyes. "I can't say that I'm surprised."

"Also, Mrs. Tolokonsky told me that her daughter Anya was infatuated with Ingall. Was that the personal issue that you didn't want to mention to me the other day?"

He stared in surprise. "I . . . why, yes. I didn't think the Tolokonskys wanted that repeated."

"Don't worry, I won't spread it around. Although, if staffers at the camp noticed her attraction to him, we may still see it as a screaming headline followed by innuendo of the crudest sort."

"Heaven help us, I hope not," said Matthias.

Matthias looked a little pale, so Nate waited for the deacon's blood to stop running cold through his veins before he asked his next question.

"What's the word on Ingall's funeral?"

"The bishop called. We'll hold it at the cathedral as soon as the police release his body. The cathedral is large enough to accommodate a crowd. Did you have a place you wanted him buried?"

"I'd like to see him in the same cemetery as my parents."

"That's a good idea. I can arrange it if you'd like."

"That would be a relief. Thank you."

"Anything I can do to help, anything for Father Ingall, I'm happy to do," said Matthias with a sad smile.

Next, Nate explained Dr. Park's solution to the children's situation.

"I'll volunteer for the trial!" said Matthias, rubbing his hands together like a child anticipating a treat.

"That's what I said," said Nate, cheered by Matthias's enthusiasm. "Maybe we can go together."

After discussing the problems of convincing the public to get vaccinated, Nate left Matthias to his work. Nate realized as he left that he hadn't told the Deacon about Loriana's burned car or the search of his hotel room. He didn't turn back. Matthias had enough information to digest for the moment. As Nate arrived back at his hotel, his phone rang. Landon Piccone, enemy of the children, was calling back.

"Hello?" Nate said as he ducked quickly into his hotel room and shut the door on the noise of a group of business travelers chatting in the corridor.

"Mr. Bryan, I don't know what you want. Although I felt your brother's advocacy of those children was a menace to public health and safety, and I'm glad he isn't around to continue spreading his misinformation, I didn't have anything to do with your brother's death."

"We'll have to agree to disagree on the value of my brother's work, Sir. I didn't call you to argue policy. I've read your record and reviewed your history. You seem much more likely to take to the legal system to attack someone than to show up and shoot them. Drawing actual blood may not be your style. However, that doesn't mean that others in your group might not support a more physical approach to gaining ground in the war of public opinion. Some have suggested that your own daughter wouldn't hesitate to raise her hand to someone with a differing opinion. I suspect that there are others in your group who advocate a more radical line of thinking on the Allergen Children. I've seen the postings calling for their eradication."

"How dare you attack my daughter! She's a child. Tolokonsky put you up to this, didn't he? If you dare slander my daughter, I will see you in court! And the same holds for Tolokonsky!"

"I'm not trying to attack anyone. I only want the truth. I'm sure you know your daughter's whereabouts for the night my brother died. Surely, a child wouldn't have been out at one in the morning. But others in your People's Health and Safety League aren't children, and if you harbor them, aid them, cover up for them, or mislead the police regarding their activities, you could find yourself charged as an accessory to murder. I want my brother's murderer found. I won't stop asking questions until I find out who killed him. It might be in your group's best interest to find the killer as well. Or do you want the public to perceive your group as fringe lunatics willing to kill to get what they want? Or, worse, as terrorists and assassins?" Nate paced the small open space in front of the television as he talked. He wished he had better powers of persuasion.

"Don't you lecture me on what's good for my group or for the public interest. I live to protect the public from this plague among us. History will show I worked to save lives. People are deceived. They see those creatures as innocent children, not as the mutant killing machines that they are. Those things are a danger to us all."

"As someone who has walked into a camp to meet with the children, I have to disagree with you. Medical science disagrees with you." Nate struggled to control his temper. "But again, my concern is solving my brother's murder. It should be yours as well, unless you want your organization to be seen as a bunch of assassins bent on stifling dialogue by killing the competition because you can't stand an honest, open debate."

"We have never been violent! *They* are the killers! The murderers! *They* are the threat to civilization!" Outrage and indignation filled Piccone's voice.

Nate fought to keep his voice even, trying not to yell back at the man, trying to keep him talking in hopes of getting any useful information out of him. "Not yet, perhaps, but your rhetoric has been getting more and more violent in its terms in recent months. In your speeches, you've said you are at war. You've called the children your enemy. You've referenced battles to be won. Even if you don't engage in violent actions, your rhetoric may be inciting your followers to take a more radical course than you would take."

"I have no intention of inciting violence!"

"Then you had better examine your language, because it could be construed as promoting extremist behavior!" Nate lost control of his temper and yelled back at Piccone.

"I'm through talking to you, Mr. Bryan. Don't call me again!" the irate Landon Piccone screamed into the phone.

The line went silent. Nate resisted throwing his cell phone across the hotel room and, not for the first time, wished for a phone he could slam down with a satisfying bang to end a call. All in all, Nate wondered what he had thought he'd accomplish by calling Piccone in the first place. If Ingall hadn't been able to reason with him, Nate's chances of holding a nonconfrontational discussion with him were nonexistent. That ended his overly optimistic dream of getting the names of the more radical members of the People's Health and Safety League out of Piccone. The police or FBI would probably have better sources and data on the fringe extremists. Would the authorities bother to check whether anyone from the People's Health and Safety League had anything to do with Ingall's death? Were the police even investigating any real leads?

Nate looked at his phone. He had a card with Detective Janwari's number on it, which another officer had given him. But he quickly decided that he wouldn't call this soon. If Janwari was actually carrying out an investigation, he was probably still focused on tracing Loriana's movements. Nate wasn't going to let him know that he was investigating his brother's murder, too. That would probably make the detective's head explode, and the last thing he needed was to create any more animosity between himself and Janwari.

As Nate stood in the room running his fingers through his thinning red hair, an idea came to him. He decided to go at the problem from another angle. With a little online searching, he could probably find a few names of the most radical people: the ones who didn't care what others thought of them and the ones who were so entrenched in the belief that they were right that they would put their names on even the most outrageous online comment. The question was how to proceed once he had some names.

Nate grabbed his laptop and flipped it open, deciding to take one step at a time. Three hours of browsing led him to the most radical of the postings regarding the Allergen Children. None of them had names attached to them, but some had emails or contact information assigned to the websites themselves. A social networking page dedicated to the eradication of the children had several hundred people associated with it. Nate culled a few names of the most vocal participants in the commentary. Studying comments attached to news articles linked to the children gave him a few more first names and screen names. Cross-referencing the names on the articles with the names from the social-media site gave him a handful of names of people who were most vociferous in expounding their views. Nate determined that several of the names might also be the contacts for the radical websites. In the end, he had names to consider but no way of knowing whether these people were all hot air and empty talk spewed on the Internet or were willing to take action.

As he was about to log off, Nate came across a message on one of the social-media sites that liquefied his spine and almost paralyzed his brain. His shoulders slumped, and he sank down in the desk chair. It read: "The time for war has come. Blind fools and sympathizers are releasing the enemy from containment. We must prevent this at all costs. We must strike before they are free to kill. The first battle for the salvation of the human race is beginning. All those ready to take up arms in defense of humanity, prepare your weapons and watch for the summons."

One of the groups was going to attack the children in the camps. Flash mobs and riots were easily organized through social media. An armed mob could descend on the camps in no time at all.

Nate sat staring at the posting, rereading it, hoping the words didn't say what he knew they said. Finally, he refreshed the page and looked at it again. The post had been viewed more than four hundred times. Aghast at the implications, he reached for his phone and turned it on. He wanted to warn someone. The attack had to be stopped. Nevertheless, short of calling out the National Guard, how could he stop a mob? Should he call the police? The camps? Could the children be evacuated to a secret location? Should he warn the Tolokonskys? Was he overreacting? Did people post this kind of thing regularly? Who would know?

Ivan Tolokonsky would know. Nate's fingers fumbled to find the right number in the contact list on his phone.

"Hello?"

"Mr. Tolokonsky, this is Nate Bryan. I was doing some research on Landon Piccone and his People's Health and Safety League when I came across a posting that worried me. It looks like someone is planning to attack the children in the camps. The message says that people will be notified soon about when and where to gather. Does this sort of thing happen a lot? Do people post messages about planning attacks regularly, or is this unusual?"

"We watch those sites for such messages. We've seen messages that looked to be planning an actual attack only once, about six months ago. The attack fell apart under additional scrutiny from the police and federal agents. Give me the address where you saw the message, and I'll have my people look into it. If it has teeth to it, any merit, they'll be able to tell."

Nate sent an email with a link to the page in question, glad Tolokonsky was taking him seriously. "Do the camps have the ability to repel a mob attack? Could additional police protection be requested? Or is it possible to move the all of the children out of the camp to a more secure location?"

"Moving all of the children at once is out of the question. They are safer where they are. The camps have better security than you might imagine. Seeing to my children's safety has been as much a priority for me as providing for their education and protecting their rights. If we find that the person behind the message is likely to incite a mob action, we will notify the police and the FBI." Tolokonsky paused. "Ah, I see your message. Let me look at the link."

Nate waited while Tolokonsky read the message he'd found and could hear him clicking and typing.

"Yes, Mr. Bryan. This does look serious. I've sent it to my contact with the FBI for evaluation. Thank you for bringing it to my attention."

"I'm relieved to know that someone will be checking it out. It made me sick to think people might attack the children in their camp."

"Thank you, Mr. Bryan. You remind me of your brother."

Ending the conversation, Nate dissolved back down into his chair, this time in relief. A glance at the time confirmed that it was time to eat something before he had to meet Loriana. Nate was no closer to solving Ingall's death, and he was emotionally wrung out. The prospect of seeing Loriana did nothing to cheer him up. Chances were he wasn't going to be happy with whatever she had to tell him.

Part of him wanted to check out of the hotel and drive back to a peaceful existence in San Marcos. However, that part was tiny and thin-voiced compared to the overwhelming anger that was beginning to fill him: anger over Ingall's death, anger over threats to innocent children, anger over his room being searched, anger over the stupidity of people who could be brought to believe clouds were made of ice cream if they'd read it on the Internet. Technology had made it too easy to make lies look true and for good people to be fooled into making wrong choices. Nate felt like throwing something or even smashing his fist into the wall in frustration, but he didn't. Instead, he collected his phone and keys and went out to find lunch.

Later, with his stomach comfortably full of greasy hamburger and wedge-cut, sea-salted fries, Nate sat waiting in front of St. John's Church. Cars passed by at a leisurely pace on the neighborhood street that the church faced. The concrete bench was hard on his rear. The humidity was high. Nate was in the shade of a large pine tree, and a moist breeze was blowing in from the south.

He'd been waiting fifteen minutes when a car turned into the parking lot in front of him. He didn't recognize the car, an older-model Ford, but the driver was Loriana. She parked with complete disregard for the lines in the lot and hurried over to him.

"Sorry I'm late. I didn't realize I was going to have to stop to get gas in my sister's car. Also, I had to talk her out of coming with me."

"Why would she want to come with you?"

"She thinks I need protection."

"You aren't in any danger from me," said Nate, raising both eyebrows in surprise.

"Not from you, no." She looked back over her shoulder and scanned the empty parking lot and open space around them.

"What is going on? Who might want to hurt you?" Nate asked, hating the pleading note in his voice, knowing she'd withheld a lot of information.

Loriana sighed with resignation, tucked her heavy brown hair behind her ears, and looked at him with large brown eyes filled with such sadness that he wanted to grab her and hold her. Nate restrained himself, looked around, and led her into the enclosed alcove of a gated prayer garden. Brightly colored annuals, red and yellow flowering hibiscus, ferns, and monkey grass filled the beds, alongside a variety of small trees, each labeled with dedication plaques marking them as memorials to the dearly departed. Small statues peeked from between the flowers. Nate and Loriana sat on a curved-backed, wrought-iron bench, warmed by the heat of the afternoon but now shaded from the sun by the side wall of the church.

Nate sat sideways on the bench, looking at Loriana, his knee brushing against her leg. She sat rigidly, her shoulders and legs aligned with both feet on the ground. She wasn't looking at him.

"What haven't you told me? What do you have that some-one wants?" Nate asked, still pleading for answers.

"The senator has been paying an informant inside the Allergen Children's Rights Movement. The informant has been giving information to the senator about the research being done and the treatment plan that is being discussed."

"So?" prompted Nate, a touch of exasperation creeping into his voice.

"So, maybe Ingall caught the informant, and the informant killed Ingall rather than be exposed. I'm not sure, exactly." Again, she shifted those sad, wet, brown eyes his way.

"Why do you think this?" Nate tried to keep his tone even.

"I overheard the senator agreeing to pay the informant. One night, a man came to the senator's house late, after mid-night. I heard them talking, but I didn't see the man's face."

"You were at the senator's house after midnight? Late-night planning session?"

Her mocha cheeks glowed lightly pink. She wasn't looking at him now. "Not exactly."

"You were sleeping with him?" asked Nate, with a flash of comprehension.

"Yes."

Nate watched Loriana's face. She was sad, tired, and maybe embarrassed, but finally she didn't look like she was being evasive or withholding anything.

"When did that start?" he asked, trying to keep any judgment out of his voice. Whom she slept with no longer interested him.

"Right after we broke off our engagement. I knew he was a rat when it came to women, but he could be charming and sweet, too. I guess he knew I was feeling vulnerable after our breakup and took advantage of my insecure frame of mind. At least, that's what I've been telling myself. Really, I have no excuse. I knew better. Anyway, the senator was a little drunk that night. After the man left, he bragged to me about how he'd found a way to slow down the research to cure the Allergen Children. A few weeks later, I heard him talking to Louisiana Senator Gilbert about payments, but I didn't know that the payments had to do with the Allergen Children."

"When Tolokonsky called to set up an appointment, you thought he was calling about the senator's affair with you?" asked Nate, seeing the picture more clearly now.

"Yes. I listened to the entire meeting between the senator and Mr. Tolokonsky. When I heard about the plan to move the kids to West Texas, several of the conversations I'd overheard suddenly made sense. I realized I had evidence of a massive plot. The next time I heard him take a call from Senator Gilbert, I recorded the conversation, in case the information was useful later."

Nate looked at her, completely taken aback, shock in his eyes. She'd collected the information, not to report the corruption but to use it as leverage on her boss if she needed it.

Loriana shifted uncomfortably under his gaze. "Then, four months later, my mom mentioned that dad had taken that allergy medicine. I sent my blood in for a test and went back to the office to search for anything related to the Allergen Children. I didn't just read what I found. I kept copies. I wasn't sure what to do with the information at that point, or even if I would do anything with it at all. When I got the results on the test for the mutation, I realized how it all affected me. I decided that I had to do something, so I called Ingall."

Nate stared into space at the individual leaves on a crape myrtle, trying not to think about Loriana's affair with Senator Coalember, her collection of corruption data for leverage, or her indecision over whether to expose the bribery she'd uncovered. Instead, he tried to put the pieces together in his head.

"So the senator was looking to profit off the Allergen Children. He was paid to propose moving them to a facility in West Texas. He conspired with at least one senator from Louisiana on that project. In the meantime, he worked to slow down research that might help the children. He did that by paying someone, someone who leaked information about the research to him, maybe even someone who broke into Dr. King's offices. Breaking into the offices didn't slow down research; it only caused security to be increased. So how did he slow things down?"

"By killing Ingall?" she said.

"That slowed down announcing the human trials. The doctors would have announced the trials already if Ingall hadn't died. You said this started months ago. Ingall was *just* killed. What was the senator doing to slow research before Ingall died?"

"I don't know. Maybe someone in the lab was tampering with results," she said.

"We need more information. We need to know if Senator Coalember is going to propose moving the children to West Texas. Tolokonsky's threats may have stopped him, but we need to know. We also need to try to find out who his informant is. The senator could have paid the informant to kill Ingall, or the informant may have killed Ingall because Ingall had caught him interfering with the research. Would you know the voice of the man who came to the senator's house that night, if you heard him again?"

"Maybe. I don't know. It's been months since I heard him." She fidgeted on the bench, finally turning to face Nate.

Nate could see the pain in her eyes. He didn't ache to heal her anymore, but he did feel pity for her for the choices she'd made.

"I'm sorry! Maybe if I'd gone to Ingall sooner, he'd still be alive," she said.

"Ingall's death isn't your fault. You didn't shoot him." Nate looked at the brick side of the church, hesitating before asking his next question, knowing that she might blame herself even more depending on the answer. "Is it possible that the senator knew that you were going to meet with Ingall? Could he have found out that you were going to Houston?"

She sighed, and tears leaked from her eyes down around her crooked nose. "My phone was issued to me by the office. If the senator was tracking my calls, he would know I called Ingall's office."

"So the senator may have warned his informant? The informant may have thought Ingall already knew his identity?"

"I don't know. I don't know." She shook her head no, willing him to be wrong.

"The day you tried to go see Ingall, he was killed. The next day your car was torched. Did you have documents or something with you to give to Ingall?"

"Yes." Her tears were flowing in rivulets down her face now, and the word came out as a gasp.

"Do you still have the information?"

"Yes. It's on a thumb drive in my purse."

Nate nodded, but didn't ask for the thumb drive. If the informant's name wasn't on anything, it would do him no good to go through the evidence of the bribery scheme. "Did Ingall know why you wanted to see him? Did you tell him that someone was tampering with the research?"

"I told him that someone was working against the children from the inside, slowing down research." She sniffed hard, pulled a wad of tissue from her purse, and wiped her nose.

"Ingall knew there was a problem." Nate paused, thinking. "He could have deduced the source of all the trouble. Knowing Ingall, he would try to deal with the person himself first. Ingall knew that he might be in danger, but he agreed to meet the person anyway. He texted me, and hoped he could reason with whoever it was."

"And the saboteur killed him. I got Ingall killed." Loriana's head sank down into her hands.

"No, it's not your fault. Ingall made his own choices, too. He knew he was putting himself in danger. You were trying to do the right thing. You couldn't predict that the senator's inside man would kill Ingall, or that Ingall would try to talk to him alone. If that's even what happened."

Silence fell between them. Nate stared into space, wondering why Ingall had put himself in danger, the floral excess around him dissolving into a blur. Loriana wept silently beside him.

Loriana pulled a tissue from her purse and dried her eyes. "I'll go back to Austin and find out whether the senator plans to propose moving the children. If anything about the informant is in his office, I'll find it. I can submit my resignation right after I find the informant."

"If the senator had your car burned while looking for any evidence you have, you'll be in danger. Be careful." Nate looked at Loriana, still beautiful even in tears, but not the woman of his dreams.

"He'll be at speaking events most of the time. I doubt the rest of his staffers have any idea that this is going on. I should be safe enough as long as I avoid the senator."

"He didn't burn your car by himself. He has someone doing his dirty work for him. Be careful. Be discreet," said Nate.

"I will."

"Will you go to the authorities with what you have on the thumb drive?" he asked.

"Yes, but not until after I find out who his informant is." She glanced at Nate, then looked away hastily.

Nate saw her look away and wondered whether she could see the sadness in his eyes, in his mouth, in his entire posture, or if she was ashamed of the choices she'd made. He changed the subject. "I found threats online. Someone may be planning to attack one of the children's camps. I told Ivan Tolokonsky, and he's looking into it."

"That's terrible! How will they protect the children?" Her husky voice cracked in distress.

"Ivan Tolokonsky says they'll be safe even if a mob attacks. He's seen to security in the building."

"Oh, thank goodness," she said.

Nate thought she sounded relieved. He wished she'd cared about the legality and morality of the situation earlier and without having to have a personal connection to it. Better late than never. He tried to keep the wry look that was twisting his mouth from his face. He would never have ignored corruption the way she had. He'd quit his previous job because, although nothing the drug company had done was illegal, it had felt unethical. Actual criminality would have driven him immediately to the authorities.

"I'll call the doctors and find out the schedule for the trial announcement and see if they suspect anyone in the lab of tampering with results. Call me if you find anything important," he said. He knew his voice was toneless, but he couldn't put the warmth back into it.

She jumped up from the bench and stood with her back to him a moment before turning slowly to look at him. A tear tumbled down one cheek. "I will. Bye." She fled from the garden, vanishing through the gate and past the side of the church. Nate heard her car door slam, the engine start, the car pull away, and then silence.

❧

Wednesday, 2 p.m., Camp Lambda.

ANYA, SANDR, SAM, and Omar stood impatiently waiting. Dr. Archepane had pulled them from their daily routine activities and left them in the lounge, telling them to wait a few moments because Mr. Tolokonsky was coming to speak to them.

Omar bounced on his toes with his hands in his jean pockets, his lips pressed together in a thin line.

"Do you think it's about the funeral?" Anya asked the others, her arms crossed as usual, looking as if she were hugging herself to calm her own nerves.

"He's probably coming to tell us that the health department won't let us go," said Sam, his acquired cynicism breaking through.

"No joke," said Oleksandr, a frown creasing his face.

The door to the lounge opened, and Ivan Tolokonsky's blue eyes glowed as he marched into the room. "It's arranged! You're all going to the funeral!" he said. "I had to pull a massive amount of strings and sign a ridiculous number of documents, as well as take out a special insurance policy, but it's done."

"Yeah!" Sam pumped one fist in the air.

"I can't believe it," said Omar. "They've only ever let us out for medical care that can't be provided here. The last time I was out of this place was for dental surgery on that tooth I broke playing basketball three years ago. Thanks, Mr. Tolokonsky! You're a miracle worker!" He exchanged a high five with Sandr.

Anya hugged her father tightly around the chest. He ran his hand down her fine blonde hair.

"Does anyone know we're going yet? The news media? Will they be willing to talk to us? To show people that we're not psycho murderers?" asked Sandr.

"I imagine the news people will be fighting for turns to get you on camera. We have to expect some unpleasant questions from them, though." Tolokonsky's eyes became serious, a line forming between his brows as he scanned the faces of the four young people around him. "The first thing the news people will do is find out who you are and whether you are linked to any deaths."

He focused on his son. "They'll ask stupid questions, like if you are sorry you killed someone or whether you think you should be sterilized to prevent the birth of others like you. They'll ask how it feels to be out in public after living in isolation. They'll ask your dreams for the future. They will ask if you are angry about your treatment. Above all, you must stay calm and patient. Don't give angry answers. Tell them you have no memory of the deaths, since you were a baby when they happened. Tell the news people that you empathize with the families who have lost loved ones. Show them the precautions you are taking to protect everyone else at the funeral—the suits and gloves you'll be wearing. After they talk to you, they'll go to Piccone and ask him how he feels to see you out of quarantine. He'll most likely say you are a murderer who should be locked up for life as a matter of public safety and then spew vitriol for the camera. You must look like the sane, reasonable ones compared to him. We need public opinion on our side."

Sandr nodded his understanding.

"When will the doctors announce the vaccine trials?" asked Omar.

"I spoke to Dr. Park. She will give a press conference a few hours after the funeral. We hope to give the public a positive look at you and then announce the treatment. People will see that you represent a medical step forward for society. That should end these stupid calls for sterilization or abortion of babies carrying the mutation, and end any ideas of imprisoning you for life!"

Anya released her father and danced happily on the spot. Omar's half smile reflected a wary optimism.

Dr. Archepane, who had been listening in the doorway to the lounge, came forward and shook Omar's hand. "It won't be long now. You'll be released to live your life," he said as he clapped one hand on the young man's shoulder.

"When is the funeral?" asked Anya.

"The diocese says it will be the day after tomorrow," said her father. The threats against the camp were in the back of his mind, but he didn't mention that. He hoped his taking the young people to the funeral wouldn't spur their enemies to act.

CHAPTER 7

Nate's Wednesday afternoon vanished in planning the last details of Ingall's funeral with Matthias, purchasing a black suit and shoes, and waiting impatiently for Dr. King to call him back. That night, when he fell into his hotel bed, Nate left his phone turned on but charging, hoping that the doctor would call. He wished he had Dr. Park's direct number. He'd left a message for her at the hospital, but had received no response.

At seven-thirty the next morning, as Nate was shaving and plotting another visit to the hospital, his phone rang. His hopes were dashed when he saw it wasn't one of the doctors but Loriana calling.

"Hello."

"Nate, the senator is dead!" she said.

"What? When did he die? How?"

"I don't know. I arrived at the office this morning and found police everywhere. He died sometime last night. The detective said he was doing a routine investigation of an unexpected death, like maybe the senator died of natural causes. The news is reporting that he was found dead in his living room by his wife late last night, with no signs of foul play."

"Did you tell them about the situation with the children and the facility in West Texas?"

"Not yet. They only wanted to talk about Senator Coalember's health and frame of mind. If he didn't die of natural causes, I expect they'll come back with more questions."

"Will you tell them everything?"

"Yes! Nate, what if someone killed him for not proposing a law to move the children? He had Tolokonsky threatening to expose him on one side, and the people who'd paid him on the other. What if the people who paid him killed him because he didn't do what he'd agreed to do?"

"It's a possibility. Don't get ahead of yourself. He might as easily have had a heart attack. Focus on why you went back there. Did you find anything to identify the senator's accomplice? Anything about who his informant might be?"

"I haven't had a chance to look yet. The police are everywhere. No one is working. Everyone is up, wandering around, talking. The senator's desk and his computer are the most likely place to look for information, but I doubt I'll be able to search today. If I tried to access his desk or computer now, someone would notice."

"All right. Stay there. See what you can find out. I still haven't been able to get a word with Dr. King or Dr. Park, but Matthias and I did get Ingall's funeral scheduled."

"When is it?"

"Tomorrow at the cathedral downtown, at ten a.m."

"I'll be there," she said.

Thursday, 7:20 a.m., Taylor High School.

"Today is the day!" said Jeanette to her core group of friends gathered at the end of an empty corridor in the high school. The bell starting classes for the day wouldn't ring for another twenty-five minutes. The halls were still mostly empty. "My second cousin inside heard that Tolokonsky got permission to take his kids to that crazy priest's funeral. The funeral is tomorrow. We can't have those murderers on the loose!"

"What time?" asked Victor.

"Eight o'clock p.m. Visiting hours will be over. Day-shift staff will be gone. Meet in the field south of the camp; bring your protective gear," she said.

"Yeah! It's about time!" said Rig, excitement gleaming in his eyes.

"Remember, my dad doesn't know about this. He's the public face of the group and has to be able to deny all knowledge of it. Don't talk to him about it. Don't tell anyone who might tell him! This is our plan, and *we* will carry it out," said Jeanette. "Text everyone else at seven-thirty p.m. That place will burn!" Her body vibrated with the intensity of her obsession.

Similar fires blazed in the minds of the teenagers as they split up and made their various ways to what they saw as dull and pointless classes. After school, they carried out the more mundane activities of the day with scant attention, their thoughts straying to the upcoming and long-awaited battle. They would be warriors, the saviors of humanity, protecting the civilian population from the plague about to be unleashed on them.

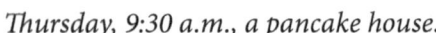

Thursday, 9:30 a.m., a pancake house.

As NATE ATE, a photo of Ingall filled the television screens on the walls around him. What had remained of Ingall's thinning, brown hair was sticking up on top of his head, and his black coat was hanging on his narrow shoulders like a jacket flung over a wooden kitchen chair. Fine stubble showed on his chin, where he'd missed patches in his haste to shave. It was an old photo but pure Ingall, slightly unkempt with an air of neglect for his personal appearance. At least his hair wasn't curling over his ears in this picture. Ingall frequently forgot to get his hair cut. Haircuts simply weren't important to him. Nate smiled for a second before the voiced-over words of a reporter knocked the breath out of him.

"This is a breaking news report. Sources inside Camp Lambda report that Father Ingall Bryan, who was found murdered this week, may have been involved in an illicit relationship with one of the children in the camp. We go now live to our reporter on the scene. Joie?"

"This is Joie Marec, here at Camp Lambda, the largest of the facilities housing the Allergen Children. Father Ingall Bryan was a familiar figure here at the camp, coming multiple times a week to counsel and teach the children who live here in medical quarantine. My source inside the building reports that, in recent weeks, Father Bryan's counseling sessions with one of the teenage female inmates had increased dramatically in frequency. My source says that the girl in question would request to see Father Bryan as often as four times a week, up until the week before he died. Then, the week before he died, Father Bryan only saw the girl once."

"Does your source think that the priest's relationship with the girl was connected to his death?" asked the anchor.

"My source won't speculate on that, nor will he release the name of the female patient in question, out of privacy considerations. However, if Father Bryan was involved with the girl, her family may have objected, leading to the sudden break in contact with the girl. Angry family members may well have exacted personal justice by killing Father Bryan rather than reporting the matter to the authorities."

"Thank you for your report, Joie," said the anchor. "We'll have more details on this breaking story as soon as we can confirm them. The funeral for Father Ingall Bryan is scheduled to take place tomorrow morning at the Co-Cathedral of the Sacred Heart. "

"Dammit!" said Nate, banging his fist down on his table so hard that a bottle of ketchup fell over and his silverware jumped. Other lunch rush patrons turned to look at him as the report on the television ended and the weather report took its place.

Nate threw his napkin down on his mostly finished meal, paid his tab, and walked outside the restaurant, fuming.

His phone rang. "Hello?"

"Mr. Bryan, this is Ivan Tolokonsky. That post you informed me about looks like a real threat. My sources report that 'chatter' has increased online regarding an attack on the camp. We expect that something may happen within the next week. I asked the police to increase security. Unfortunately, all they will agree to do is increase the number of patrols in the area. They don't want to dedicate a car to the facility. They feel the threat is still too ambiguous to warrant that sort of response."

"What about federal protection?"

"The FBI agrees that the chatter has increased, but won't go so far as to say an attack is imminent on any particular camp. They want to try to figure out which camp in which state might be targeted."

"So what do we do?" asked Nate.

"Keep listening to the chatter to see if we can isolate a specific threat."

Tolokonsky's calm response surprised Nate. "That doesn't seem like enough," he said, disbelief in his voice.

"My children are in there. Believe me when I say that they are well protected." Tolokonsky's voice turned sharp.

"Of course. I'm sorry. You've overseen security." Nate paused. "Have you seen the garbage the media is spewing about Ingall?"

"Yes, I saw. Someone has started a smear campaign. They think by discrediting him in death they can discredit his work." Ivan Tolokonsky sounded unfazed, as if he had expected such tactics.

"The source is said to be at the South Houston camp," said Nate.

"A former staff member, a member of the cleaning or laundry service, or someone fired for poor performance trying to take revenge, most likely." His tone of voice dismissed the source as unimportant, a distraction in the face of larger matters.

"What if it's someone still working there? What if the disgruntled employee is working with those who might attack the camp? Could an employee help a mob into the facility around the security measures?

Ivan was silent. "Inside help could give attackers floor plans, the layout of the complex, but little more. Staff would be aware of the monthly safety drills, and that the drills have the children move to the cafeteria at the center of the building. However, most employees would not be fully versed in the systems protecting the cafeteria."

"I have time this afternoon. Do you mind if I go ask questions at the camp about the source of the report about Ingall, just in case the person is still working there?"

"You may do as you wish. I have arranged for four of the children to go to the funeral. I have many details to handle today in order to ensure their safety and that of the public. We can have no accidents. Let me know if you find the source of the report."

"Okay," said Nate, knowing that the source would be fired in a heartbeat and likely never hired within the city of Houston again, if Tolokonsky had anything to say in the matter.

～

Thursday, afternoon, Camp Lambda.

"Mr. Bryan, how nice to see you again. What brings you back to the camp today?" said Dr. Archepane, his white hair combed straight back from his forehead, reminding Nate of a white lion mane.

"Have you seen the latest news reports on Ingall?" asked Nate.

"I didn't bother to read the articles. I didn't have to go beyond the titles and first sentence to know that the reports are total fabrications. There was no inappropriate relationship between Father Ingall and a patient. He would never have done such a thing. It wasn't in his nature." The doctor spoke calmly, reassuringly, not realizing that Nate hadn't come for reassurance.

"I'd like to find the source of that story. The news suggested that the source works in this camp. Mr. Tolokonsky and I have found evidence that someone may be planning an attack on one of the camps. If someone is willing to lie about Ingall in order to hurt him and his work here, that person may be willing to help someone attack this camp."

"I was informed of the possibility of a threat to the camps in general. Do you really think that we may have a traitor here?" asked the doctor, his eyebrows raised.

"Yes!" said Nate forcefully. He wanted the doctor to see the potential danger they were facing.

"Most of our employees are carriers of the mutation. They are sympathetic to the children housed here and would never conspire to harm them." The doctor's white eyebrows were drawn together in concentration, giving the matter thought.

"Most, but not all?" prodded Nate, waiting for more information.

Dr. Archepane pondered the question a moment before speaking. "Everyone working here had to undergo a background check and interview. The news reporter may have been tricked into believing the source of the story worked here when, in reality, they didn't."

"Wouldn't the reporter have confirmed employment as part of a fact check before accepting the story? She wouldn't just take the source's word, would she?" Nate pointed out what he thought would be a basic requirement for journalism.

"That would probably depend on how inexperienced or dumb the reporter was. Nevertheless, you're right. An editor would insist on some kind of verification before airing such a story. We have to assume the person works here or did work here recently." Anger and disappointment chased each other across the old doctor's face.

"Very recently, given that the details of the story covered Ingall's visits here right up to his death," said Nate.

"Come with me," said Dr. Archepane with decision. "We can look into this." He led Nate down the hall to a door marked "Human Resources."

After a three-and-a-half-hour search, before which the doctor had summarily dismissed the head of human resources with the words, "You don't want to know what I'm doing, so take the afternoon off," they'd identified three possible sources for the story about Ingall. Since the facility was staffed around the clock, with certain nonmedical workers on eight-hour shifts and medical personnel on twelve-hour shifts, only one suspect was at work. The other two had not arrived yet.

"Wait here, Mr. Bryan. I'm going to have a word with Jorge Reynoso. He works security in the parking lot," said Dr. Archepane. He moved swiftly around the desk at which he'd been seated and out of the room. Nate was struck by the youthfulness and speed of the doctor's movements.

After spending so much time with the doctor, Nate was aware the man had to be somewhere between sixty and eighty years old, but he couldn't have guessed his age any more precisely. The doctor's thick mane of hair was not prematurely white. Age spots on his arms and the texture of the skin on his face showed him to be nearing retirement. However, the doctor's energy as he worked and his evident zest for his profession gave Nate the feeling of being in the presence of a much younger person. All the same, Nate began to wish that he'd accompanied the older man, to back him up if he needed assistance.

Fifteen minutes later, to Nate's relief, the doctor returned unharmed.

"It's not Jorge," he said.

"You're sure?" said Nate.

"Very. I spoke to his coworkers and his manager in security before I spoke to him. He isn't a carrier of the mutation, but his girlfriend is. His girlfriend has a younger sister in one of the Louisiana camps. Jorge wouldn't leak such a story about Father Ingall. He had met Father Ingall and liked him. He thought the story was completely invented. I'm pretty good at detecting lies, especially when I'm looking for them. I don't think Jorge was lying to me." Dr. Archepane stood with his arms crossed on his chest. "You have the funeral tomorrow. Do you need to leave? I can deal with interviewing the other possible sources of the story when they come in for the shift starting at six tonight."

"The funeral planning is done. Ingall's assistant, Deacon Matthias, is handling the last-minute issues. I wanted to speak to the children again, if I could."

Dr. Archepane glanced at this watch. "It's four-thirty now. We have time before dinner. The kids will be in their afternoon study-hall period. If you can find the way yourself, I'd appreciate it. I have a meeting with the county health department shortly, and I don't want to have to go through decontamination."

"Sure," said Nate.

The doctor tossed Nate a pair of thin protective gloves and directed him toward the lounge.

The babble of voices that poured over Nate as Dr. Archepane opened the door to the lounge indicated that the students weren't getting much studying done.

Nate took a moment to find Omar and the Tolokonsky kids in the crowd.

Nate approached the group. "Hi, how are y'all doing this evening?" He nodded to Sam, Sandr, Anya, and Omar.

Omar looked up and smiled at him. "Mr. Bryan, hi." He stood and shook hands. "We were just discussing leaving this place tomorrow for the funeral. While we wish it wasn't for Father Ingall's funeral, we're excited to be seeing the outside world. I've only seen the inside of a church online or on television."

Nate said, "Ingall would be glad to give you a reason to leave this place. Although, I'm sure he would have preferred to live to see you walking free."

"How long will the funeral last, Mr. Bryan?" asked Anya.

"Probably over an hour in the church, with another half hour or so at the graveside."

"We leave at nine o'clock. The funeral starts at ten. We shouldn't have to come back here until noon!" said Sandr happily. His eyes widened with excitement.

"Or maybe later," said Omar.

Nate hated to change the subject, but he thought the kids might have noticed if someone working in the facility seemed mean or unsympathetic. They might have an idea who had leaked the story about Ingall to the press. "Have you seen the news today?"

The smiles vanished, and anger sparked in Sandr's eyes. "Yeah, we saw the filth someone is spreading about Father Ingall," said Sandr.

"Can you think of anyone here at the camp that would spread a story like that? Someone who works here and knew when Ingall visited, someone who might want to harm you and your cause?"

Anya, going pale and then pink in her cheeks, shook her head, as Omar squinted his eyes in consideration.

"We never see some of the staff. They don't have contact with us. The people we interact with on a daily basis would never spread such a story," said Omar with intelligent concern in his eyes. Nate could almost see his brain analyzing the possibilities.

"Don't worry about it. Dr. Archepane is looking into it," said Nate.

Ms. Jemington's voice rang out over the babble of voices, announcing the end of the study hour. Nate said his goodbyes as the teens collected books and belongings scattered about them.

Showered, changed, and decontaminated, Nate walked back to Dr. Archepane's office, uneasy about leaving the older man to interview more suspects alone. It was almost six p.m. At the very least, he could stay and hear the results of the interviews, if the doctor wouldn't agree to let him listen.

Nate found the doctor in his office with personnel files stacked neatly on his desk.

"Mr. Bryan, I thought you'd left," said the doctor in surprise.

"I was going to, but I wanted to ask if I could sit in on your interview of the last two suspects. If one of them is helping the people who are plotting to attack, he might be dangerous."

The doctor looked at Nate with consternation. "Surely that isn't likely. In all probability, none of our employees is involved, and the whole story was fabricated. After all, the members of the media are aware that Father Ingall didn't carry the mutation. Exactly what kind of illicit relationship could he carry out without being able to make physical contact? We don't have virtual reality sex programs or any other software-driven devices of that nature at the children's disposal. Anything that crosses to the children's side of the building has to be decontaminated before leaving. The protocols are quite rigid. The more I consider the matter, the more idiotic it seems."

"I know, but someone knew when Ingall was here and who he saw. If that person is aiding those who want to hurt the children, if they know how to bypass security here, then an attack on this facility could be much worse. Someone willing to help do that kind of damage could be extremely dangerous when confronted."

"But we have no proof that an employee is involved in any of that! Besides, the staff members that are conversant with the security features here have been fully vetted."

"I understand that. All the same, I'm worried," said Nate, pressing the point.

"If it will ease your mind, come with me. We'll talk to the last two employees on the list," said the doctor with a placating smile.

"Thank you," said Nate with relief.

Thirty minutes later, they tracked one of the employees to an equipment and machinery room, where he was doing maintenance on a water heater. The man was kneeling down in front of the heater with an open tool box at his side.

"Patrick Finn?" said Dr. Archepane.

The man looked around quickly. "Yes? Oh, hello, Doctor. What can I do for you?"

"I need to ask you a few questions. Do you have a minute?" said the doctor, politely.

"Sure, Doc." The man laid his tools aside and wiped his hands on a towel as he approached Nate and the doctor. He gave Nate a curious glance, but turned his attention to Dr. Archepane.

"Did you hear that scandalous story released today regarding Father Ingall Bryan and a patient in this facility?"

"Yes," said Mr. Finn with a chuckle. "Stupid story."

"Do you have any idea who the source of that story might be?" asked Nate.

Mr. Finn stopped smiling abruptly, taking in the serious expressions on Dr. Archepane's and Nate's faces. "Well, it wasn't me!"

"Relax, Mr. Finn," said the doctor. "We aren't accusing you of anything."

"Good! I'm late shift. I don't know what hours Father Ingall was keeping or how often he visited. I figured someone made that part up, but if you're here questioning me, I guess someone got those details right."

"Forgive me, Mr. Finn, but you are one of the few employees here who don't carry a mutation. What brought you here? Most noncarriers fear the mutation too much to even walk into the building, let alone work here."

"I'm the one nonmutant in my family. Both my parents carry one copy. So do my two siblings. My niece was born with the double mutation. I may not be a carrier, but I sympathize with them. They are people, and they deserve rights like everyone else. I came here because the position was open, and I wanted to do something to help."

"Thank you, Mr. Finn. If you had to speculate, do you know of anyone on our staff who could have released that story to the press?"

"No, Sir, I don't. It would have to be someone who could check the visitor logs and knew when Father Ingall visited." He paused, then added with a look of disgust, "Someone with a nasty streak."

"Thank you for your time. We'll leave you to your work," said the doctor.

Walking down the hall, Nate asked, "Does the last employee on the list have access to the visitor logs?"

"Yes. Tullis Johnson cleans the offices on the administrative side of the building. He could have logged onto a computer to sneak a look at the records when he was in an office to vacuum or empty the trash."

Dr. Archepane and Nate searched the administrative offices that were now dark and empty. The time was well past seven-thirty when they gave up searching. They'd asked several people on the evening crew, and none had seen Tullis Johnson that evening. He apparently hadn't reported for his shift.

Nate considered it suspicious that the man hadn't shown up, but Dr. Archepane took a lighter view.

"He's probably sick. Most likely, he has family who carry the mutation but doesn't happen to be a carrier himself."

"If he isn't the source of the story, how did the person who made up the story know when Ingall was here?"

"I don't know," said Dr. Archepane, "but there's nothing more we can do tonight."

"I suppose not. I've kept you long enough. Goodnight, Doctor."

The doctor walked Nate to the exit. Nate sat in his car in the nearly empty lot. A few cars remained. Some family members might still be in decontamination processing. Others might be spending the night with their children.

Nate was driving down the road leading away from camp when he noticed cars pulling slowly into a nearby field. He slowed his car as he drove by. People were parking and getting out of their vehicles. Some carried bats. A few had rifles. The sun had set, but darkness had not yet fallen. In the twilight, Nate couldn't be sure how many people moved around the cars and under the trees.

"Damn!" he thought as he swung his car around and drove back toward the camp. As he reached the parking lot, a wall exploded in front of him. He was too late.

Nate could see a mob of people marching down the main entrance road toward him. He didn't want to risk trying to get into the building. If someone were to open the door for him, the mob might get inside, too. He couldn't drive through the mob, but staying in his car in the parking lot might be suicidal. His eyes scanned the area and found a maintenance track probably used by utility vehicles to service the buildings. A single hanging chain between two concrete posts blocked the road. Nate jumped out of his car and found that the chain was easily removed. He undid the chain and sped his car down the utility road to the back side of the building.

With the building between him and the mob, Nate felt safer, but he could no longer see what was going on. The sound of bullets firing filled the air. Smoke rose in the evening sky.

To Nate's ears, it sounded as if a war were being fought just out of sight.

He picked up his phone and tried to call Ivan Tolokonsky, but got no answer. Frantically, he dialed 911 and requested assistance, but didn't remain on the line as instructed. He tried to call Ivan Tolokonsky again. Briefly, the thought passed through his mind that Tullis Johnson's absence that night was well-timed.

Chapter 8

Thursday, 8 p.m., Camp Lambda.

"The others are here," said Rig.

"How far back are they?" Jeanette asked as she looked over her shoulder, trying to see into the darkness beyond the well-lit parking lot.

"Close. They're in that field beyond the parking lot."

Jeanette watched and saw the crowd moving toward them in a swarm, looking like a single, enormous, living creature sweeping toward them in the twilight. As they'd been directed, the crowd members wore whatever they felt they needed to protect themselves from the dangers outside the building: gloves, rubber boots, hip waders, and bulletproof vests. She nodded in satisfaction as she surveyed them.

Jeanette and her crew wore full Mission Oriented Protective Posture, or MOPP, gear, including rubber gloves and overshoes, purchased from a military surplus provider. The two-piece outer garment, called a JSLIST and manufactured in El Paso, could protect against chemical, biological, and radioactive contaminants. Since they hoped to breach the building as far as the mutant murderers' living quarters, Jeanette wanted all the protection she could get. Jeanette, Rig, and Victor had each purchased their own set of gear. They'd opted to get only the protective gear without any gas masks or respirators, partly for budgetary concerns and partly because the secretions that could kill them weren't airborne.

When the approaching crowd reached just the right distance away, Jeanette said, "Now!"

"3, 2, 1," said Victor. He pushed the button.

They crouched low, waiting for the force of the blast and the deafening sound wave to hit them. The information available on bomb-making on the Internet had been more than sufficient for their needs. Their device was fertilizer-based, powerful, and detonated by a cell phone. All they'd had to do was place it at the base of the wall.

An instant later, the wave blew over them, knocking Jeanette over from her crouched position onto her side and pelting her with bits of concrete. She righted herself, glad of the earplugs she'd thought to bring but removing them now. Out of the corner of her eye, she saw the crowd flinch as one, hesitate, and then spring forward with a roar like a battle cry. They were coming to back her up. She exulted, adrenaline coursing through her veins. Finally, she would get justice.

Victor and Rig were already sprinting forward toward the break in the wall. She followed as quickly as she could through the pile of broken brick and rubble. Dust filled the air, clogging her nose and burning her throat. Ahead of her she could see Victor had thrown his first bottle, but it shattered against the window, spattering gasoline against the outside of the building. The window hadn't broken as expected.

Rig pulled out his gun and fired four shots at the glass, but still it didn't shatter.

"Throw more bottles and light them anyway! Try all of the windows!" Jeanette screamed over the sound of a shrieking alarm.

Jeanette tried all the doors along the courtyard, but none would open. Rig fired six rounds at the door lock. Two bullets found their mark. He kicked hard, and the door flew open into a hallway. Jeanette joined him and they entered the building.

Red alarm lights were flashing, and the shrieking of an alarm pulsed through their ears. Racing down the hall, they came to an open area with exercise equipment. An interior door at the end of the room led deeper into the building, but it was locked and appeared to be made of steel. They must have activated some kind of fireproof or blast-proof door.

Frustrated and unable to proceed, Jeanette moved back from the door, with Rig following closely behind her, and pulled another bottle from her backpack.

Rig lit it and Jeanette launched it uselessly at the door.

Rig lit and threw another at the room full of exercise equipment, setting fire to a treadmill. They retreated into the hall, lit three more, and launched them, leaving the entire room of equipment ablaze. As thick smoke filled the hall, they moved back toward the door they had used to enter the building. They would do as much damage as they could in the area they could access.

Seeing nothing but smoke and the glow of flames, Jeanette and Rig sprinted back to the courtyard, flinging the last of Jeanette's bottles behind them. Fires burned all around. Another door stood open and smoke poured from it. Victor, with his shotgun, had gotten into the building, too. Jeanette was having trouble seeing through the smoke to find the way back to the parking lot. Rig vanished in the haze. Gunshots rang out. Jeanette heard a bullet zip by her head and ricochet off the wall behind her. A light breeze blew, clearing the smoke momentarily. She saw the rubble around the break in the wall and ran to it.

Police and fire engine sirens wailed. Jeanette could see the flashing red and blue lights speeding down the main road to the camp.

"Everyone get out of here!" she screamed.

A few people nearby heard her and turned to look at the approaching emergency vehicles. They began to run, scattering in all directions.

Jeanette broke into a hard run. She was panting, her lungs aching, as her feet pounded across the parking lot. She leaped through the row of bushes planted around the lot into the field where they had left the car.

She covered the quarter mile to the car, which had been left parked behind a vine-covered, forgotten barbed-wire fence.

Rig sat inside, covered in soot and panting heavily.

"Go!" she said as she slammed the car door shut behind her. Her chest was heaving, her breath coming in hard gasps. Her hands and knees shook as she fumbled for the seat belt.

"What about the others?" he asked.

"I don't know where they are. The police are here. We have to go now!"

"But . . ." he said as he started the vehicle.

"Do you want to be arrested?" she yelled.

"No, but . . ."

"Then drive! Now!" she screamed.

He looked into her wild eyes and knew better than to try to argue with her. Rig threw the car into gear and began to turn it just as Victor appeared from the shadows.

"Wait for me!" He stumbled against the car, blood seeping down his right arm and dripping from his fingertips. His left hand was clasped over his upper right biceps. Blood oozed between his fingers. He used his bloodied left hand to open the car door, revealing a large gash in his right arm.

Rig drove the car across the field with his lights off until he came to a road. He urged the car up a small embankment onto the road, flicked on the lights, and drove as fast as he dared away from the flashing lights and sirens surrounding the camp.

∾

Thursday, 8 p.m., Camp Lambda parking lot.

Elizaveta sat on Karim's lap in the back seat of his car. His hands ran through her silky blonde hair and then moved downward to her tiny waist.

They only had a few more minutes. The camp doors were locked, and her parents would be expecting her to arrive at home soon. She'd had to argue with them to let her ride with Karim to the camp. If she got home late, they would say "no" next time she asked.

A huge blast shook the car.

"What was that?" she asked, jumping from his lap and twisting to look out the back window of the car. Smoke and dust were rising from a section of the wall at the edge of the parking lot. She could just see three people climbing over the rubble and into the camp's contained grounds.

"Look! Over there!" said Karim, pointing the opposite way, toward the road.

Elizaveta swung around to see a crowd of people flowing toward the camp. "We have to stop them!" She started to open the car door.

"Are you crazy? We can't stop that many people!" He grabbed her arm and held her in the car.

"We have to do something!" she screamed, desperate for action, hitting at the hand that held her back.

"Call 911!" he said.

She fumbled for her phone, dialing frantically.

"Help! I'm at Camp Lambda! Someone blew up a wall. A mob is attacking the main building!"

The dispatcher spoke calmly while entering the call. "Please stay on the line. Police and fire departments are on their way."

"Send lots of police. There are hundreds of people!"

People flooded into the parking lot carrying guns, pipes, and Molotov cocktails. Many began firing their weapons at the building and at the few cars in the parking lot. The cars in the lot belonged to night-shift staff members and to family members staying the night at the camp. The sound of bullets striking the cars and glass shattering filled the air.

"They're shooting at us!" she said to the dispatcher.

"Keep your head down!" said Karim, grabbing Elizaveta and pushing her to the floor.

"I have to call my dad!" she said, hanging up on the 911 dispatcher and dialing. "Daddy! The camp is being attacked. We're trapped in Karim's car in the parking lot! People are shooting at us!"

She couldn't hear his response in the chaos.

"I can't hear you. It's too loud. I called 911. The police are coming. Help, Daddy!"

Ivan Tolokonsky yelled into the phone loudly enough for Karim to hear his response. "I'm coming! Keep down. Stay in the car."

The glass from the side window shattered. Elizaveta screamed and dropped the phone. She slumped to the floor.

Ivan Tolokonsky stared at his phone. "Hello? Eliza!" He yelled her name, but she didn't answer. The call ended. Suddenly the phone rang again. "Eliza!" he yelled.

"No, this is Nate Bryan. I'm at the camp. It's under attack!"

"I know. Elizaveta and Karim are still there. They are stuck in a car in the parking lot. People are shooting at them!"

"I'll go look for them," said Nate.

"I'm on my way there now," said Ivan, ending the call.

∾

INSIDE THE CAMP, Dr. Archepane and Ms. Jemington raced from their own quarters as alarms sounded. Dr. Archepane had just settled down to read the latest copy of the *New England Journal of Medicine* on his tablet. Ms. Jemington had finished her final rounds, gone through decontamination, and checked exterior locks after having seen the last of the visiting family members out of decontamination only moments earlier. She'd sat down in her room and kicked off her shoes when an explosion shook the building.

"Yes, send the police now!" Ms. Jemington yelled into her phone over the sound of the alarms. "Something exploded!"

She met Dr. Archepane at the end of the corridor. "The police are coming," she said.

"We need to move the children to the cafeteria now!" he said.

Together they sprinted to the dormitories, where they found the evacuation in progress. The night staff, a few parents, and the teenagers were carrying the smallest children in their arms while driving a small pack of grade-school-aged children ahead of them.

Protocol for an emergency, which they'd practiced in monthly drills, called for moving everyone to the windowless cafeteria and sealing the doors with everyone inside. The room had its own ventilation system, fireproof doors, and reinforced walls, in addition to food, water, and medical supplies. Mr. Tolokonsky had spared no expense in creating an extremely large "panic room."

Ms. Jemington, in her stocking feet, went with the children to the cafeteria, speaking calmly, reassuring the children as they walked.

Dr. Archepane remained at the dormitories, double-checking rooms as they emptied and locking them behind him.

The acrid smell of gasoline and smoke hit his nose. Black billowing clouds crept around the corners along the ceiling and into the dormitory hall. He could see smoke seeping around the door that led to the exercise area and to the outdoor sports courtyard. Red flames leaped behind the small shatterproof glass window in the door.

"Cover your nose and mouth with your shirts and stay low!" the doctor said. He heard the sound of breaking glass and knew that attackers had infiltrated the building itself. He prayed that the security doors between sections of the building had locked automatically and held the invaders back.

As the doctor reached the toddler room, Omar and Sandr emerged with two night-care nurses. Each carried two little ones, ranging in age from twelve to twenty-three months. Dr. Archepane was always amazed by how small children could sleep through the alarms, but most had awakened now because of the blast, the alarms, or being picked up.

"Is that the last of them?" he asked.

"Yes," said Omar. "This is the last trip."

"Go! I'll do the final check. Let Ms. Jemington know she can do the final head count," said Dr. Archepane. He watched them hustle away, balancing their sleeping charges. The smoke in the hallway was getting heavier. He coughed hard, ducked down, and entered the toddler room. Empty cribs and toddler beds lined the walls. He checked under and around each, moving blankets as he went before deciding that no one had been left behind.

Returning to the hall, Dr. Archepane closed and locked the door. He coughed hard and realized he could no longer see the end of the hall through the smoke. Dropping on his knees, he began to crawl along the corridor, covering his nose and mouth with his shirt as he went.

In the cafeteria, Ms. Jemington completed her count. Eighty-four children and teenagers were all accounted for. Ten parents held their own kids. Thirty staff members looked after the crying and scared children, as the teenagers held and comforted the three- to five-year-olds who had awakened to find their world in chaos. Only Dr. Archepane was missing. If he didn't appear within the next minute, according to protocol, she would have to seal the last door without him.

As she walked to the control panel for the door, Omar jumped to his feet and ran to her.

"Dr. Archepane isn't here yet!" he said.

"I know, but we can't endanger everyone else. We have to seal the door."

"Give him one minute!" Omar grabbed her arm to hold her back.

"I can't!" she said, shaking off his hand.

Omar opened the door and looked down the corridor, hoping to see the doctor. When he didn't, he stepped out the door.

"Then give me one minute," he said. He sprinted down the hall, back toward the dormitories, without waiting for her answer.

"Wait!" Ms. Jemington said, but he was gone.

Sandr saw Omar leave and ran to join Ms. Jemington.

She stared at the second hand on her watch, counting to fifteen, then thirty. She looked out in the corridor as the tiny hand hit forty-five seconds. When she started to close the door at fifty seconds, Sandr put his hand out to block her.

"Wait. He's coming," said Sandr.

They heard Omar's voice yell out. "We're here!"

Ms. Jemington peeked around the door and saw Omar supporting Dr. Archepane, half dragging him down the hall. Sandr ran to help Omar with the older man. Together, Omar and Sandr dragged the doctor into the cafeteria.

The doctor collapsed onto the floor. Ms. Jemington hit the button to seal the door.

Dr. Archepane coughed violently, folding at the waist. The smell of smoke drifted through the air around him, wafting from his hair and clothes.

"He needs oxygen!" said Omar.

"It's with the medical supplies," Ms. Jemington said as Sam appeared next to them with a large medical kit.

"I've got it!" Sam said, popping a mask over the doctor's face.

KARIM SAW ELIZAVETA go limp. He couldn't see her injury in the shadows, but knew she must have been shot. He put his hand under her head to lift it onto his lap and felt the warm stickiness of blood.

He pulled his hand back and looked at it. His palm was shiny and dark. He knew it must be red, but it looked murky in the yellow light of the parking lot.

Bullets stopped pummeling the car. The crowd had moved past the parking lot and was focused on the building itself now.

Karim could smell smoke in the air and see the orange glow of flames nearby, but didn't dare lift his head to see what was burning. He was pretty sure his car wasn't on fire, but one of the ones parked near him might be. He stared down at Elizaveta's silent form. Was she breathing? He realized that she must have been shot. He put his hand under her head to lift it and felt the warm, slippery wetness of blood. The bullet that had broken the window must have ricocheted and stricken Elizaveta in the back of the head.

He leaned over her face, putting his ear to her mouth and nose, and felt warm air hit him. She was alive. He stripped off his shirt and wrapped it around her head, holding his hand over the bloody spot. If only she would wake up. Now that he knew she was alive, his fear began to subside and anger began welling up inside him.

He heard sirens sounding. Help was coming.

People began to run by the cars, fleeing the approaching authorities.

The bubbling anger became rage. Karim didn't want any of them to get away. He wanted them all caught and sent to jail for what they'd done. He wanted to hurt them all, but he couldn't leave Elizaveta.

He stayed down on the floor, cradling her head, until he heard a knock at the window. He looked up to see Nate Bryan staring in the window.

"Help me. She's been shot!" Karim said.

Nate and Karim carried Elizaveta away from the crowds toward the maintenance road where Nate had left his car. They laid her down on the ground behind a towering pine tree. Karim cradled her wrapped head in his lap, seated with his back against the tree, a brown carpet of pine needles beneath them.

"Stay here," said Nate. "I'm going to get help." He ran toward a fire truck pulling to a stop in the parking lot.

A moment later, Nate returned with a paramedic who opened his kit and began to examine Elizaveta. As they were moving her to a stretcher, Karim heard a loud, familiar voice yelling "Elizaveta! Karim! Where are you?"

Karim looked around to see a policeman trying to prevent Ivan Tolokonsky from coming closer to the building.

"Over here!" he called, waving his arm.

The policeman released Mr. Tolokonsky, and he ran forward.

~

Friday, 3 a.m., Camp Lambda.

AROUND THREE IN the morning, Nate Bryan and Ivan Tolokonsky left Vera Tolokonsky at Presbyterian Hospital, watching over her unconscious daughter, and drove back to the camp. Nate had called Detective Janwari, but the detective had been terse in their conversation. Janwari wouldn't come to the camp. Nothing involving the camp had been assigned to him, he had said, because it had nothing to do with his murder investigation. Nate had ended the call completely disgusted by the man's response.

Police vehicles still blocked the road. The men had to stop for clearance before police allowed them to pass the barricades and drive toward the building. Yellow police tape marked off the hole in the wall leading to the play area. Scorched areas of brick splotched the building in the light from the tall lamp posts in the parking lot. The burned-out shell of a car stood in the lot. Ivan's eyes strayed to the car in which his daughter and her friend had been hiding. Bullet holes riddled the trunk. The windows showed multiple bullet holes. Elizaveta had been lucky. The ricocheting bullet hadn't hit her at full force as it had tumbled through the air. Her skull had been fractured and she had a concussion. The doctors had placed her in a medically induced coma for the time being. However, the doctors were optimistic that the damage would heal.

Nate and Ivan Tolokonsky had returned to the camp to evaluate the damage and see the children. Both men knew that Dr. Archepane had been taken to Presbyterian Hospital to be treated for smoke inhalation and that none of the children in the camp had been physically injured. However, they needed to make a decision. Should the four teenagers still be allowed to attend the funeral in seven hours? Or would it be too dangerous for them? Were they too shaken by the attack to face the crowds and reporters?"

Ivan needed to see Anya, Sandr, Sam, and Omar before he made up his mind. Now, it seemed even more important to humanize them in the press, after such an attack, so that people would understand the enormity of it and not just shrug it off. Would the children have the strength to go through with it?

Inside the building, Ivan was pleased to see that the security features had mostly worked. The attackers had managed to breach two exterior doors, but the interior safety doors had held, so the damage to the interior was relatively minimal. The exercise room was a sooty, soggy shell, with charred pieces of ruined equipment lying haphazardly everywhere. The contents of a storage closet had burned, as had several offices in the halls near the exercise room. Although the invaders had been unable to break through the safety doors to the dormitory hallway, the smoke had seeped through. The ceiling around the dorms was soot blackened and smelled strongly of gasoline and smoke, but the rooms themselves were intact and the children had returned to their beds. The cafeteria's panic-room systems had functioned admirably.

Stopping only for Nate to put on gloves, they wove through the halls to reach the lounge. Here, they found Omar, Sam, Sandr, and Anya waiting for them. Anya drowsed on the couch, curled on her side with her knees to her chest. Sam sat with his head down on his crossed arms at one of the tables.

Omar, soot marks still on his face, paced as Sandr watched him from his seat on the couch near his sister's side.

Seeing his father, Sandr leaped to his feet. "How is Elizaveta? How is Dr. Archepane?"

At his words, Sam lifted his head, Omar stopped pacing, and Anya stirred and stretched before sitting up.

"Elizaveta is unconscious still, but the doctors don't expect any permanent damage," said Ivan, wrapping his arms around his son tightly before releasing him and moving to his daughter. He then moved to hug Sam and Omar in turn. "Dr. Archepane has suffered some minor smoke inhalation. They will observe him overnight and most likely release him in the morning. I understand you saved his life," he said, looking at Omar, who gave a sheepish half smile. "Well done!"

"He should have been right behind me. The smoke overcame him. I had to go back for him."

"It's okay," said Ivan. "Now, we must discuss the funeral."

"We want to go," said Sandr decisively, his eyes intent and defiant.

Nate looked at him, studying Sandr's eyes before looking at Omar, Sam, and Anya. They looked exhausted but determined. "If that's going to happen, y'all need to get some sleep. Once the reporters start in on you, you'll need to think on your feet. No one can think fast when they haven't slept."

Ivan peered through frowning eyes at his daughter, who looked, thin, pale, and vulnerable to him. "You don't have to go, you know. I can take the boys only."

"I'm going! For Father Ingall!" A tear leaked out of the corner of her eye.

"Then you need to sleep. Go to bed now, all of you," said Ivan. "We have more to discuss, but it can wait until morning."

After the young people filed out of the room, Nate said, "Are you sure they should do this?" The shock and trauma of the evening would still be fresh tomorrow.

"It's now or never. While I regret that it is for your brother's funeral, I have been waiting for a good excuse to bring a group out of the camp. They need to be seen in public!" said Ivan.

Nate nodded. "Before the attack, I was with Dr. Archepane. We were trying to determine who might have given that story about Ingall and a patient to the press. We eliminated two of three suspects, but couldn't find the third employee, a man named Tullis Johnson. He apparently skipped work tonight. He may be sick or something, but, given the circumstances, I find his absence tonight suspicious."

A murderous look crossed Ivan Tolokonsky's face. A chill went down Nate's spine as the look vanished, replaced by a mask of concerned interest. "I'll look into Mr. Johnson's whereabouts," said Tolokonsky through clenched teeth.

Nate felt compelled to remind him that the man might not be involved at all. "Johnson could be innocent."

Tolokonsky nodded that he'd heard the comment.

"What about the announcement from Dr. King and Dr. Park?" asked Nate, changing to a safer subject.

"Dr. King wanted to delay again, saying the announcement will get lost in the coverage of the attack and the funeral. He may be right, but I don't want to wait any longer. Dr. Park has called a press conference for three o'clock at the hospital."

"I'll be there," said Nate.

They finished their tour of the damaged areas of the building and walked to decontamination. An hour later, Nate stumbled back into his hotel room, exhausted, hoping that nothing more happened before the funeral and the press conference. He didn't have the energy for another emergency.

CHAPTER 9

Friday, 8 a.m., hotel.

The next morning at eight o'clock, Nate's ringing phone awakened him. His alarm went off a fraction of a second before the phone began to ring. He'd only managed to get about three hours of sleep.

"Hi, Mr. Bryan?" came a strong, confident female voice. "This is Dr. Michaela Park."

"Hi, Dr. Park. What can I do for you?" Nate rubbed the sleep from his eyes and tried not to yawn into the phone.

"I was hoping you'd be willing to stand up with me at the press conference for the announcement of the vaccine. I had expected to have Father Ingall by my side. Would you be willing to stand in for him?" she asked. "I meant to ask you before, but I couldn't find your number. Then I got the message you left yesterday."

Nate smiled to himself, a half-hearted, crooked smile. He'd never be able to fill Ingall's shoes, but he could stand up in his place for this. "Yes, Dr. Park. I'd be happy to stand with you during the press conference."

They settled on meeting at two-thirty p.m. in Dr. Park's office. From there, they would proceed out together to face the press corps.

"Will Dr. King be with you, too?" Nate asked.

"I have some bad news about that. We're not supposed to talk about it, but I'm sure someone will leak it to the press soon enough. Dr. King was injured during another vandalism incident here at the hospital about half an hour ago."

"Is he okay? What happened?" asked Nate.

"He will be fine. He's bruised, and he had an asthma attack. I found him on the floor of my lab half an hour ago. Papers were scattered all over the place and equipment thrown around. I'm still cleaning up. Dr. King heard something when he arrived this morning and went to investigate. He interrupted the vandals, and they knocked him down. The shock of it triggered his breathing difficulties. He's being examined in the ER, but he says he is fine. I'm hoping he doesn't miss the press conference. He's been the leading researcher for the children for the last two decades. Most of the information we have on how the condition developed, we owe to him. I could never have come up with my vaccine idea without his work. In spite of that, I don't want to delay this announcement any longer. I've told him that if we have to proceed without him, we will."

"Dr. Park, someone inside the hospital is responsible for this. You have a traitor, a mole, someone paid by a senator to disrupt research. I think that person may even work in Dr. King's lab."

She gasped in surprise. "How do you know this?"

"It's a long story; I'd rather explain it in person to both you and Dr. King. I'll come before the press conference and tell you all about it. Okay?"

"Okay. I don't think you can be right, though. After the vandalism incidents, everyone was investigated, from the lab assistants down to the janitors. But I'd like to hear what you think."

"See you soon," said Nate. He unwrapped the black suit he'd purchased for the funeral, laid it out, and headed for the showers. He wondered whether asking him to stand by her in Ingall's place was Dr. Park's way of trying to pull him into research with her. If it was, he wasn't entirely sure if he minded or not.

A short time later, Nate sat down and prepared a short statement to give in case the press asked him any questions at the funeral or press conference. He would tell them that Ingall had meant to volunteer for the vaccine trials and that he'd happily take Nate's place. He, of all people, understood the risks of such a trial. As far as informed consent went, he was the most informed consenter ever. He would take a stand for the children. Would he work with Dr. Park, too? Should he quit teaching and leave the university for full-time research at the hospital? Nate still didn't have that answer.

～

Friday, noon, cemetery.

THE FUNERAL MASS had lasted an hour and a half, with the Co-Cathedral filled to capacity. A large police presence surrounded the church. Dark-suited officers and FBI agents checked the bags and identification of everyone entering. The heavy security was well-organized, however, and didn't delay the start of the funeral itself.

The graveside ceremony was a mere twenty minutes. As it ended, with Nate, Sandr, Anya, Sam, and Omar each tossing a flower on top of the casket, Omar found himself wishing the ceremony wouldn't end. He'd never spent so much time in such a wide-open space before. The cemetery was huge, with rows of marked graves extending for hundreds of yards in all directions. The sky was a pale blue with puffy white clouds over head. The air was warm and damp. For that moment, the day felt beautiful, peaceful, and free, a sharp contrast to the madness of the night before. Omar was exhausted. He hadn't slept at all, but he wasn't ready to go home to bed yet.

The priest intoned the final blessing, and people began to move around, unfrozen from the positions they'd been holding during the interment. Whispered conversations began as groups formed. Some people drifted from the edges of the groups toward the parking lot.

Ivan Tolokonsky gathered his waiting charges and urged them to start walking toward Nate Bryan. They each shook his hand. He smiled at them and thanked them for coming. Then Ivan moved the teenagers toward the cars waiting to return them to Camp Lambda, while Nate stayed behind to speak to a waiting group of mourners.

As they reached the edge of the graveyard itself, the teenagers came to the cemetery office building and chapel. They rounded a corner to the parking lot. Voices yelling and cameras flashing stopped them in their tracks. Reporters, possibly hundreds of them, lined the sidewalk between the cemetery and its parking lot. A few reporters moved forward suddenly, as if instinct told them to shove a microphone in their targets' faces, but they jerked to a halt, keeping their distance.

"They're afraid of us," Omar said under his breath to his friends.

The reporters' questions were flying in from all directions. Omar couldn't make out any coherent questions in the jumble of voices.

"One at a time, please," he said, giving them all a confused smile.

A shout rose up above the others. "Are you sorry for the deaths you caused?"

"Seriously?" replied Omar, a look of distaste on his mouth. "Our home was attacked last night by a mob of maniacs. A chunk of it is still smoldering this morning. A girl is in a coma, and a man almost died. And you ask us about something we have no memory of? All accidental deaths are a tragedy, but it may surprise you to know most of the people in our facility did not cause any deaths. Their mutations were identified through testing at birth. We are not murderers and criminals. We have never intentionally hurt anyone. We will always work to ensure that no one is hurt or killed by the chemicals on our skin, just as we did today. We are innocent people who want to live our lives freely."

"What are your names?"

"I'm Omar Yassine."

"I'm Sam Nganadomi."

"I'm Oleksandr Tolokonsky."

"I'm Anya Tolokonsky."

"Tell us about Father Bryan. Did he ever behave inappropriately toward you?" called another voice.

"Absolutely not! Father Ingall was great! He would never have behaved inappropriately with any of us!" said Sam.

"What about the reports we've heard about repeated inappropriate contact with a female patient at the camp? Did Father Bryan meet with female patients individually? Did he spend time alone with anyone?"

"Father Ingall provided individual counseling for anyone who needed it, male or female. Counseling and therapy sessions are private, but private does not mean inappropriate," said Omar.

"So he did spend time alone with female patients?" yelled the voice.

"STOP!" yelled Anya. "How dare you imply such things about Father Ingall! You pretend to be reporters. You claim to report the news! You are a bunch of gossip mongers! I asked Father Ingall to come to see me at the camp! I did! He never would have done a thing like you . . . you . . . idiots have been implying!"

"Why did you ask for him to see you?" asked a female reporter, inching closer but keeping her distance.

"I was having anxiety attacks. How would you feel if you lived every day of your life in a cage, unable to leave, monitored constantly while people who don't know you and never bothered to meet you debated your fate? Debated whether you would ever live freely or ever be allowed to have children? Talked about you as if you were some animal that had to be spayed? Father Ingall cared about us. He came to teach us, to advise us, to help us. He was a trained psychologist. He came to help me learn to control my anxiety, to help me find a way to deal with my insomnia."

Sandr interrupted, "Father Ingall could have died if he'd laid an unprotected finger on any of us, but he came to see us anyway because he believed in us. You'd rather spread rumors about a dead man and ruin his reputation, now that he's no longer here to defend it, than tell the truth. Father Ingall cared for all of us. We miss him." He was angry and feeling the loss of Father Ingall more than he had previously, the funeral having brought finality to the situation.

Multiple reporters began shouting out questions. Sandr heard the name Piccone in the cacophony of voices and guessed someone was asking about the deaths of Piccone's children, but ignored the question. Next to Sandr, Anya burst into tears, her lovely face red in the cheeks and the tip of her nose. Tears slid down her cheeks and fell on the dress she wore over her protective body suit. Sandr put his arm around her shoulder and hushed her.

Sandr had to take several deep breaths to keep his voice under control. He said, "We are tired. Most of us were up all night because our home was attacked. Our doctor almost died of smoke inhalation. My youngest sister was shot and is in a coma. We've lost a friend and mentor to murder.

Father Ingall was killed because he stood up to those who would deprive us of our rights and treat us as if we aren't human. Father Ingall saw us as we are, and he came when no one else would. He wasn't afraid of us. He was kind, intelligent, and devoted to showing everyone our treatment has been unjust."

Nate Bryan came around the corner behind them and came to a stop next to Ivan Tolokonsky. The reporters saw him, and the jumble of shouted questions began again.

"Mr. Bryan, Mr. Bryan, why did you go to your brother's home the night he died?"

"I went because I was afraid something was wrong. And it was."

"Mr. Bryan, can you comment on reports that your brother had an inappropriate relationship with a female patient?"

"Those reports are lies."

"Why do you think your brother was killed?"

Nate looked at the reporters, wondering if they were as dumb as their questions. "Many people are trying to present these children as dangerous and deranged killers who ought to be imprisoned for life or even euthanized. They've characterized Ingall's work to help the children regain their rights and their place in society as a threat to public safety. Any number of people might have wanted to kill him out of fear and ignorance. I think Ingall was killed for doing the right thing for these young people." Nate moved forward and put his hands on Anya's and Omar's shoulders. A frenzy of camera flashes blinded him.

"Mr. Bryan, do you carry a copy of the Allergen Mutation? Are you immune to the toxin they secrete?" called a voice.

"No. I'm not immune, and neither was my brother. These young people have worked hard to ensure my safety. I trust them."

"Do you think that the attack on Camp Lambda last night is related to your brother's murder?" asked an earnest young woman with a microphone, who had slowly inched toward them, breaking from the pack of other reporters.

"I have no idea, but it does reflect the violent rhetoric and the rising hysteria surrounding these young people," said Nate.

"Do you know anything about the press conference being called at the medical center this afternoon about a research breakthrough for these children?" the woman asked.

"I do. I intend to be at the press conference, but I'll leave the explanations to the doctors. Look, these young people are tired. They need to go home," said Nate, ending the question-and-answer session.

"Please, let us through," said Omar as he led the others toward the reporters.

The crowd parted before him, unwilling to get close as the teenagers passed through. The reporters were still afraid of the young people, but some were looking them in their faces and meeting their eyes. Cameras zoomed in on the teenagers' expressions, lingering on Anya's beautiful, tearful face.

Friday, 1:30 p.m.

NATE SAT IN his car in his black suit and debated what to do next. He pulled off his tie and unbuttoned his collar. Suits and Houston's humidity did not go well together. Nate had snacked on finger foods at the post-funeral reception at the church and downed only one very weak cup of tasteless coffee while he received the condolences of hundreds of people. The press conference at the hospital was in two hours. Nate was exhausted, but he had heard rumors of arrests for the attack at the camp. He needed a real caffeine kick and a place to browse the Internet. Nate drove to a coffee shop, bought a double espresso, and sat down at a table. He flipped open his tablet and started looking for news related to the attack on the camp.

Word had circulated after the funeral that Landon Piccone was being questioned about the attack on the camp. Nate found multiple articles about the attack, skipping over the early unreliable reports and clicking to open one headlined "Jeanette Piccone, daughter of Landon Piccone, arrested." The article stated Jeanette had been taken into custody after the car she had been riding in was pulled over for speeding by police three miles from the camp. The driver of the car and Jeanette were arrested, and a third person was taken to a hospital with injuries. All three were covered in soot and smelled of smoke and gasoline. Two guns were found in the car along with three sets of military-grade protective equipment called MOPP gear.

Nate felt sure security camera footage would show that all three had taken part in the attack on the camp. The next article included quotes from Landon Piccone. He was denying all knowledge of the attack. He claimed his daughter and her friends were attending a movie, not attacking the camp. When asked how one of the teenagers with his daughter had become injured at a movie, Mr. Piccone blamed police brutality. When asked about the gun found in the car, he'd claimed it had been planted there to frame his daughter. Thirty other people had been caught fleeing the camp. Police were still trying to trace who had organized the attack. Additional suspects were being sought. Anyone with information was asked to contact police.

The next article in the series detailed texts and social-media posts used to organize the mob attack on the camp. The article quoted sources implicating Jeanette Piccone as a primary suspect in planning the event. Police withheld comment on the ongoing investigation. A defense lawyer laughed at the suggestion that a fourteen-year-old girl could have planned such an assault. A quasi-opinion article suggested a link between the attack and Ingall's murder, but contained only speculation and supposition, no fact of any kind. As Nate read, a new article detailing the funeral popped up. He skipped that article. He'd been there. He didn't need to read the summary.

His phone rang. Loriana was calling. Nate realized he hadn't seen her at the funeral. Where had she been?

"Nate, I'm so sorry I missed the funeral," said Loriana. "Some tests must have come back on the senator. The police came to my house last night to ask a ton of questions and told me not to leave town this morning."

"They think he was murdered?"

"Since they're asking about recent threats he'd received and who his enemies were, I'd guess so," she said with a huff of annoyance.

"Did you give them the recording and the papers you kept?" Nate ignored her huffiness.

"Yes. I told them everything. They seemed skeptical that it could be linked to Ingall's killing, since the senator and Ingall were on opposite sides of the issues politically."

"It's not that big of a stretch, but I'm not surprised. The authorities there probably don't want to deal with the Allergen Children any more than the authorities here do." Nate paused in thought. "The person who killed Ingall could have killed the senator. Or someone from the construction company could have killed the senator for backing out on their deal."

"The police think I'm overreacting, trying to connect the two deaths because I knew both victims. The scenarios linking the deaths may be too complex for the detective to consider likely. Police want a simple answer."

Nate could hear disdain in Loriana's voice. "They don't suspect you, do they?" he asked.

"I don't think so," she said slowly, thinking about it. "If they do, they're being very circumspect about their questioning."

"Landon Piccone's daughter has been arrested in connection with the attack on the camp, but I don't think she was involved in Ingall's death. Somehow, I can't see Ingall agreeing to meet a fourteen-year-old girl outside his home. He'd have put her off until daytime and held the meeting somewhere public. Ingall knew the person who killed him well enough to allow his killer to come to his home at night. I could see Ingall agreeing to meet Landon Piccone privately, but not his daughter."

"Was Landon Piccone at the attack on the camp?" she asked.

"I don't think so. He apparently has an alibi for the attack. I wonder if his daughter could have set up the whole thing without his knowledge. Ivan Tolokonsky thinks she has the brains and the drive to do it."

"Having been one myself, I'd say not to underestimate the deviousness or intelligence of a fourteen-year-old girl," said Loriana with a laugh.

"At least we can be sure that the senator wasn't on her radar," said Nate.

"I still don't have any idea who the senator's mole was. If I find anything, I'll let you know."

"Okay," said Nate. "I'll be at the press conference at the hospital this afternoon. I'm going to tell the doctors about the traitor in their office."

"Okay," said Loriana. "Do you still plan to volunteer for the trial?"

"Yes."

"Hmm," she said.

Nate wondered what she was thinking, but didn't ask. Instead, he said goodbye and hung up. He finished his espresso, checked his email and messages, and left for the hospital, hoping the caffeine worked quickly.

Friday, 2:30 p.m., Memorial Hermann Research Center Hospital.

NATE ARRIVED AT the hospital research building, having passed the usual graffiti and the dripping black messages calling for the Allergen Children's freedom. He found several police cars in front of the building, officers standing inside in small groups talking, and the security man at the desk even more alert than usual.

Nate presented his identification and was subjected to a metal detector before he was allowed to go see Dr. Park and Dr. King. Perhaps the hospital wasn't taking any chances of violence breaking out during the press conference.

The door to Dr. King's suite was propped open. As he approached it, Nate could hear unhappy voices raised in discord.

"I'm fine. We are NOT cancelling that press conference," said Dr. Park in a vehement voice as Nate came in the door.

"What happened?" Nate asked.

The people gathered in the room all turned at once, startled by his voice. Dr. King and Dr. Park stood at the center of a small group of people that included two EMTs and several young men and women who looked to be lab assistants. Dr.

Park held an ice pack to her right wrist. One EMT was closing up his equipment case, preparing to leave.

"You really should get that x-rayed, Ma'am," said the EMT, apparently reiterating a point already discussed.

"I know. I know. I will," said Dr. Park. "Thank you for your help."

The EMT nodded and left the room with his partner, passing Nate as he went out into the hall.

"What happened?" Nate asked again.

"I fell," said Dr. Park.

"You didn't fall, you were almost killed!" said Dr. King. "We can't go on like this. Someone will be killed. We can release a written announcement of the plan. We don't have to stand up in front of the press like so many targets for the shooting."

"Willett, we are not going to be shot. We are going to have the press conference, and we will do it verbally. This is too important to be announced with a memo!" said Dr. Park, her tone like reinforced steel.

"Please, tell me what happened!" said Nate, stepping into the battle of wills forming in front of him.

"Someone tied fishing line across the stairs. I always use the stairs instead of the elevator. My foot got caught on the line, and I fell down a flight of stairs. My wrist is sprained and I bruised my knees, but I'm FINE." Dr. Park's green eyes sparked. The firm line of her jaw was set. Locks of her brown, silky hair slid down to her shoulders, having escaped from a clip that had held it on her head.

"Your wrist could be broken. You should have it checked!" said Dr. King, firmly and loudly.

"After the press conference!" retorted Dr. Park. She stomped her right foot hard. Dr. King stepped back, his hands up in surrender, frustration in his eyes.

"Who did this? Do you have any ideas? Are there cameras on the stairs?" questioned Nate.

"Whoever did it knew the camera had a blind spot. We have video of dozens of people using the stairs. Most of us use them since the labs are spread over the third and fourth floors. It's faster than waiting for the elevator. Also, it isn't unusual for groups to stand talking on the landings or wherever they happened to meet on the stairs, discussing different parts of the same project," Dr. King said.

"Are you sure you're okay?" asked Nate, glancing back at Dr. Park as she winced when she moved her hand.

"Yes! I'm not going to let a bunch of idiots stop me from announcing the biggest medical breakthrough of the century! Come hell or high water, we're having this press conference. I don't care if I have to go with my arm in a sling or if they have to wheel me to it on a gurney."

Nate grinned at the look of challenge on her face. Her chin tilted up as she looked down her nose at him.

"I'm not going to disagree with you!" he said, amusement gleaming in his eyes as he fought back a crack of laughter. "Did anyone call the police? This needs to be reported."

She smiled back at him, all of her even, white teeth showing and her green eyes flashing. "Let me take some ibuprofen and comb my hair and I'll be ready for the conference. We can report the matter to the police later!" She pushed a silky strand of hair out of her face and back behind her ear.

"Dr. Park, I've got ibuprofen in my desk. I'll get it for you," said a red-haired young man in a lab coat.

"Thank you, Zack. I appreciate that." Dr. Park smiled at the young man, who blushed across his pale cheeks as he left the room.

Dr. King called the rest of the people in the room to attention, clapping his hands. "The rest of you, you can go down and take your places before the press conference starts. But please be aware of your surroundings. Keep your eyes open for anything around you that looks suspicious. Until today, we've only had minor incidents here, vandalism and such. Today's incident upped the ante. Whoever is doing this is getting more desperate to stop us. It doesn't seem like they have the ability to mount a more sophisticated attack. Security here is very good. But that doesn't mean a less-sophisticated method couldn't cause real damage," Dr. King said.

Nate looked at the faces of the people in the room. Most were somber. A few were angry and ready to fight back. Dr. King himself was clearly shaken by the incident. Nate thought that if Dr. King had been the one to fall, the damage might have been much worse. He was older and less flexible than the younger Dr. Park.

The red-headed Zack returned and placed a small bottle of pills in Dr. Park's hand. Popping the lid off, she shook out two pills, dropped them in her mouth, closed the bottle, and tossed it back to the young man. He caught it in one hand and shoved it in his coat pocket.

The group of postdoctoral lab workers dispersed, moving out the door to the hallway.

"Dr. King, Dr. Park, I have some information you need to hear," Nate said.

"Is this about our vandal?" asked Dr. Park.

"Yes."

"What's this?" asked Dr. King.

"My former fiancée, Loriana Montilla, works for Senator Coalember. Or *worked*, I should say. You might have heard on the news that he was found dead. Anyway, Loriana overheard the senator talking to a man about your research here at the hospital. That man was paid by the senator to interfere with your work, to try to slow any progress that might help the Allergen Children."

"Does she know what he looks like?" asked Dr. King, sinking down into a desk chair, looking pale.

"No. She heard his voice, but she never saw his face," said Nate.

Dr. Park shook her head in anger. "Why? Why did the senator want to block our progress?"

"The senator was paid to propose a law to move the children out of the cities to isolated, prison-like facilities in the middle of nowhere. He was profiting off their isolation. If you resolved the medical issues, he'd lose money, and so would the company backing him."

Dr. Park growled like an enraged pit bull. "Those greedy bastards! I don't know who the traitor could be here at the hospital, but when I find him, he'll have to answer to me! I can't believe someone would do that!"

The blood had completely left Dr. King's face. Nate feared the older man might pass out. "Are you all right, Dr. King?" Nate asked.

"Yes. I'm shocked. Just shocked. Most of my team has been with me for years. I can't imagine any one of them taking money to . . . to . . . do what? Contaminate studies? Change results? What did this person do, exactly?"

"I'm not entirely sure," said Nate.

"We'll have to have everyone vetted again," Dr. Park said.

"Yes," said Dr. King in a broken, dispirited voice.

"Did you see anything to hint at who the vandal was this morning, Dr. King?" asked Nate.

"No. Whoever it was must have heard me coming and hid behind the door. I was hit over the head from behind as soon as I stepped into the room."

"Excuse me, Dr. Park, the conference will be starting soon," said Zack, the lab assistant. He was poking his head in the door.

Dr. Park glanced at the clock on the wall. "Thank you, Zack." Zack's red head vanished around the door frame. "We should get going. I need to make myself decent, but I want to discuss the problem of our attacker some more," said Dr. Park.

Nate wondered how long the red-haired young man had been standing outside the door. If he hadn't left with the others, he had probably heard everything Nate had told the doctors.

"If someone is being paid to harm us, you'll be a target standing there in front of the press. Please reconsider. We could hand out the press release and skip the live announcement," said Dr. King, pleading with Dr. Park.

"No!" said Dr. Park. "This is too important!" She turned on her heel and left the room.

Nate followed Dr. King down to a large, square, bare room. Microphones were set up over a podium on a platform. A dozen reporters stood chatting, working on their phones or laptops, or checking video and sound equipment. As he watched, even more reporters flooded into the room. The conference would be well covered by the media, probably because it fit in with the other big news events of the week: Ingall's death and the attack at the camp.

Dr. King surveyed the room and shook his head. "I'm not sure we should do this today. Vandals this morning, booby traps on the stairs this afternoon. Who knows what they'll try next!"

"Whoever did those things is probably trying to get the news conference delayed. We shouldn't give in to those threats. We'd be doing exactly what they wanted."

"I suppose. All the same, I think a press release would work and keep us all safe."

"Yes, but the press will give a live announcement better coverage. Questions will be asked and answered. A press release wouldn't have the same impact," said Nate.

"The method of announcement won't change the value or importance of the message," said the doctor.

"No, it won't," said Nate. "But we need good strong press to get the ball rolling on this. We need to win over public opinion."

"I know, but at what cost?" said the doctor. He turned and walked away, his shoulders slumped, his cheeks still pale.

KARIM YASSINE LEFT Presbyterian Hospital in a smoldering rage. Elizaveta was still unconscious. He'd only been allowed to see her for a moment before her mother had pushed him out of the room again. The news was reporting Jeanette Piccone's arrest for involvement in the attack on the camp. Karim wished he could get his hands on her, but she was still in police custody.

He wanted revenge. Those Piccone people were rotten excuses for human beings. They were trying to send Omar to prison, and they'd almost killed Elizaveta. He wanted to stop them.

Karim wished he had the double mutation. He'd go to their house and rub his hands all over the door knobs. That would take care of them. If only he could. Then, an idea hit him.

What if he took something from the camp? Something like a used glove or a worn shirt? He could rub that on their door, and it would have the same effect. How would he get it out of the camp? He'd have to smuggle it through decontamination.

But how? He'd need time to think that out. There had to be a way.

∽

Friday, 6 p.m., hotel.

SITTING IN HIS hotel room a little later, Nate recalled the gasps among the press corps as Dr. Park had explained the solution to them. He hoped the gasps translated into prime placement on all the news sites online and on the television news hours. When the news conference had ended, most of the reporters were frantically calling editors. Any of them who'd only sent a single reporter without a video crew was regretting that choice.

Nate hoped supporters would jump on the bandwagon quickly. They would need all the positive support they could get. Nate would have to wait for the stories to come out to see how the various news organizations spun the facts. Would they be skeptical? Would they hail the solution as the answer everyone had been hoping for? Would they disparage the vaccination as dangerous to the population? Perhaps it would come down to each reporter's bias or each editor's point of view.

For most of the press conference, the reporters had focused on Dr. Park. Dr. King had stood behind her, nervous but present. She had answered question after question regarding the trials and the potential to cure so many diseases. She'd emphasized the leap forward in medicine that the trials represented. That the children would be free to return to society had been almost a side note. Dr. Park had done a good job explaining how the mutation studies had led to a breakthrough that would help all of humanity.

Nate had been allowed to fade into the background until a reporter had asked whether Dr. Park thought it would be difficult to get volunteers for the trial. Dr. Park had explained that their first volunteer had been Father Ingall Bryan. That had brought the reporters' attention back to Nate. He'd confirmed that Ingall had volunteered and said that he was willing to volunteer in Ingall's place. Among the shocked faces in front of him, he noted a few looks of respect. He hoped he had looked solid and sane, not like a man willing to risk his life on a whim. The more normal he looked, the more people might be willing to take a chance on Dr. Park's plan.

As he ate dinner in his room in front of his television, Nate flipped channels back and forth to get an idea of the media response. What he saw was encouraging. All of the stations aired video of the teenagers leaving the funeral, including shots of Nate with his hands on their shoulders. They looked like any other teenagers. Clips of their responses to questions were played.

But the big news wasn't that the children had attended the funeral. The medical news was making the biggest waves. So far, three stations were cautiously optimistic about Dr. Park's plan. One was openly skeptical. Another was proclaiming her work to be the medical breakthrough of the century, worthy of a Nobel Prize. Most channels included a review by a medical correspondent who could only say that the study results looked very positive, but that the human trials still had to be completed. Several wondered whether volunteers could be found who would be given a condition that could potentially be deadly to others. Another reporter thought volunteers would be easy to find among families of those suffering from ailments that could potentially be cured. Nate thought that was most likely true. How many people would jump at the chance to eliminate cancer and autoimmune disorders?

Nate gave a satisfied sigh of relief and wondered how Loriana was doing. He needed to find out whether she'd made any progress in identifying the senator's source in the hospital. As he picked up his phone to call her, a title on the television screen caught his eye, and he stopped to read it. It said, "Senator Proposes Moving Allergen Children."

The announcer said, "In an odd twist of timing, at almost the same moment the doctors in Houston, Texas, were explaining their possible solution for the matter of the Allergen Children, Senator Gilbert from Louisiana was proposing a bill in the senate regarding the children. The bill proposes moving the children to isolated facilities, away from major population centers, in the interest of public safety. Given the medical announcement made today, such a move may be found to be unnecessary."

Nate's tensed shoulders relaxed. If everyone took this wait-and-see attitude, they would be okay. No one was going to want to incur the extra cost of building new facilities and moving the children when a possible solution to the issue was at hand. The lawmakers' ability to put things off as long as possible and the individual states' desire to keep budgets intact would be a help instead of a hindrance for once. Thank God Dr. Park had insisted on going through with the press conference. If she'd postponed, the evening news anchors might instead be proclaiming the importance of moving the children for the sake of public safety.

The next story came up. The anchor reported that the death of Senator Coalember had been ruled a homicide. The senator's autopsy results showed lethal levels of a common heart medication in his blood. The senator hadn't been prescribed the medicine, and none had been found in his house. Law-enforcement officials had refused to discuss the ongoing investigation. The anchor did report that the grieving widow had a strong alibi, having been halfway across the country for a charity event at the time of the senator's death. They didn't connect the death to the Allergen Children's situation at all.

None of the law-enforcement agencies involved seemed to want to believe any of the attacks or deaths could be connected to Ingall. Nate had called Detective Janwari about the attack on Dr. Park, but the detective had said that it was a new issue, not connected to Ingall's death. Someone else, someone not working in the homicide department, would be assigned to investigate. Nate wondered why he had bothered calling the police. It seemed he was the only one who could see that it was all connected.

Nate clicked the television off and dialed Loriana's number.

"Hello?" answered Loriana.

"Hi, it's Nate. Did you find out anything else about the senator? I saw on the news this evening that he died of a lethal dose of heart medication."

"Federal agents are investigating now. I've had to repeat everything about four times to agents from different branches of law enforcement. I think one agency is investigating the murder, and another is looking into the bribery accusations. The senator from Louisiana who proposed moving the children today has no idea what kind of trouble he's facing. Mr. Tolokonsky may be getting a visit from federal agents, too. They were really interested in the meeting he had with the senator. They think Tolokonsky could have killed the senator to prevent him from proposing laws that he saw as harmful to the children, but I think they're wrong. Tolokonsky could have simply exposed the bribery scheme rather than kill the senator."

"So you've had no chance to look into who might have been feeding the senator research information?"

"With this many agents around? Not a chance. But I did pick up one useful bit of information. One of the agents asked me if Senator Coalember had been sick recently. When I said that he'd seemed as healthy as ever, they asked if he had any reason to be exchanging calls with someone at Hermann Memorial Research Center Hospital in Houston."

"Well, that's confirmation of the source's location anyway. I don't suppose they had a phone number that went to a particular office?"

"I think the number on the senator's phone went to the hospital's main number. He'd have to have gone through the system or an operator to be transferred to whomever he was calling."

"Another dead end," said Nate. "Dr. Park and Dr. King were both attacked today. Dr. King was hit from behind and had an asthma attack when he found someone vandalizing Dr. Park's office, and Dr. Park fell on a trip wire on the stairwell. Fortunately, neither of them was seriously hurt. Most likely someone was trying to stop the doctors from presenting their solution for the children at the press conference. Dr. King wanted to postpone the press conference, but Dr. Park insisted on going forward with it."

"Wow," said Loriana. "Maybe that will help solve Ingall's murder. The police will investigate the attacks on the doctors. They might find the senator's source. If whoever attacked the doctors is the source, and we can link that person to Ingall, we might have our murderer."

"I'll go have another talk with Dr. Park and Dr. King. Ingall agreed to meet this person at night, so it must be someone he knew. Maybe the doctors noticed if Ingall was talking more with anyone in particular in the lab. The doctors both have a handful of people working in their labs. Dr. Park said they'd all been vetted, but I think they need to do a more in-depth look."

"Hmm, I wonder . . . What do you think this person thought they would gain by attacking the doctors today? The research will go on, even if they are hurt or killed. The breakthrough has been made. Other doctors would step in to continue the studies. At most, someone could only slow things and keep them at the status quo for a short while longer." Loriana paused, thinking. "I don't see the point. The states aren't going to want to move the kids now that a solution has been put forward. What did the attacker want to accomplish?"

"Well, the idea of moving the children might have gotten more traction today if the medical announcement hadn't come out. People might have felt moving the children was a reasonable idea," said Nate.

"Yes, but that would have changed tomorrow or the next day when the medical news came out. They couldn't have expected any long-term results from postponing the announcement." Loriana sounded perplexed.

"I see what you mean. Maybe when we find who, we'll understand why. The motive could be anything. For all we know the person only wants to hurt the Allergen Children any way they can: by hurting the doctors working for them, by delaying work that could help them. Someone like Landon Piccone or his daughter would see any little delay as worthwhile," said Nate.

"I suppose," she said. "All the same, I feel like we're missing something key."

"We're missing all sorts of information," said Nate. "All we can do is keep looking."

"All right. I'll keep trying to find something on this end. If anything turns up, I'll call. If I don't find anything here in the next day or two, I'll come back there. If I walk through the labs at the hospital and listen to people, maybe I'll recognize the voice I heard talking to the senator."

"If you think that would work, we can try it. I'll run that by the doctors as well."

"Nate, Dr. King is the lead researcher, right? Dr. Park is newer," said Loriana, her voice thoughtful.

"Yes, why?"

"You don't suppose Dr. Park could have hampered Dr. King in order to upstage him? To replace him or have her research completed first? Could she do that?"

Nate paused in thought, picturing the intense and driven look on Dr. Park's face. "Dr. Park is a very motivated and focused researcher, but I can't see her vandalizing the labs. She's built her work on Dr. King's. Besides, the voice you heard talking to the senator was male."

"She could be working with someone else. And she's succeeded where Dr. King didn't. We know someone was tampering with things in his lab. Maybe she did it to stop him and give herself an advantage."

"I guess it might be possible. But then, why would someone set a trap for her on the stairs?"

"She could have staged that to draw suspicion away from herself."

"I saw her today. The injury looked real to me."

"Well, she is someone Ingall knew well. He might have agreed to meet her at night. It's your investigation. If you think she's not involved, I'll take your word for it." She cleared her throat, her husky voice softened. "By the way, I saw the press conference on television. You were great."

"Thanks. All I had to do was stand there. Hard to screw that up."

She laughed a deep-throated chuckle. Nate noticed his heart didn't leap the way it once had at that sound. Maybe he was finally over her. A twinge of sadness swept through him.

He almost missed hearing her say goodbye, but responded quickly in kind and hung up.

Friday, 6 to 8 pm (visiting hours), Camp Lambda.

KARIM'S MOOD WAS dark, but he plastered a fake smile on his face, hoping no one else would notice. He didn't see how everyone else in the lounge could be celebrating. Father Ingall was dead, murdered. They'd all been attacked by a crazed mob less than twenty-four hours ago. Elizaveta was in a coma. But no one seemed to care about any of that. They were too busy focusing on the fact that the news had shown the Tolokonskys, Sam, and Omar at the funeral and that people were interested in the treatment plan Dr. Park had created. So what if the public suddenly cared? They would change their minds again, or forget in two weeks. The best way to bring real change in the world was revolution. Karim knew that. He'd studied history.

While everyone else ate desserts from the impromptu party, Karim studied the room. He'd brought a cloth table napkin from home draped over a plate of cookies. The cookies had been consumed, and he held the napkin in his hands, playing with it. He went around the room with it hidden in his hand, wiping over the back of a sofa. He pretended to wipe the table clean with it, removing invisible crumbs from the space before him. He had his weapon prepared.

Now, he just had to get it through decontamination. He would take it in the shower with him inside a plastic bag. Yes, that would work. Then, it wouldn't be taken away with his clothes. Most of the decontamination process was a voluntary procedure in which visitors and staff worked to make sure that nothing dangerous left the building. People entered the showers from one side, leaving any contaminated material behind, and exited through the other side to the clean room. The showers were powerful and followed a programmed series of washing and soaping, sort of like a car wash, but more thorough. If he could find a way to keep the napkin near the ceiling, part or all of it might escape decontamination. The napkin might get wet, but that shouldn't remove all of the secretions from it.

From there he could walk right out of the building. No one would frisk him or double check that he wasn't taking anything with him. He could get the napkin out of the building unsanitized.

But, but, but. He stared at Omar's intelligent face and realized some of the DNA would trace back to Omar. He couldn't lead the police straight to Omar! They would lock him in a prison first and ask questions later.

Karim tossed the napkin in the nearest trash can and considered his options. He would get revenge for Elizaveta. Landon Piccone and his family would pay. How, though? His eyes fell on the empty cookie platter. The cookies had been peanut butter chocolate chip. He had his answer—an untraceable way to make Landon Piccone suffer.

CHAPTER 10

Saturday, 9 a.m., Memorial Hermann Research Center Hospital.

At nine the next morning, Nate arrived at the hospital to meet with Dr. Park. He'd called her the night before after talking to Loriana. Dr. King hadn't answered, so Nate had left him a message. Dr. Park had agreed to meet Nate again without hesitation, which he took as a sign in her favor. Loriana's suggestion that Dr. Park might be the killer had lodged itself firmly in his mind. Other than the fact that he liked her and that it would mean more than one person had been involved in tampering with the research, Nate had no real reason to exclude her as a suspect in Ingall's death. All the same, Nate was struck again by her intelligence and enthusiasm for her work. He looked forward to seeing her.

After being cleared by the security receptionist in the lobby, Nate took the elevator to the third floor, where Dr. Park's office was located, a floor below Dr. King. Exiting the elevator, Nate noted an odd smell in the air. Smoke. He wondered for a brief flash of a second whether someone had lit a cigarette, in violation of hospital policies. Alarms began to sound, shrill and deafening, ringing through the hallway.

Nate ran toward Dr. Park's office. The smoke grew thicker. As he reached the door, he found it propped open, smoke pouring from the room. Nudging the door the rest of the way open with his shoe, Nate tried to peer in through the heavy smoke. Flames were engulfing a desk.

Nate crouched down and yelled into the room. "Dr. Park! Are you in here?! Dr. Park!"

Covering his mouth and nose with his shirt, Nate crawled through the door, scanning the floor for anyone. He spotted a woman's comfortable, black leather walking shoe near the burning desk and scrambled toward it. The flames were leaping upward, burning a wall that the desk was butting against. The ceiling began to burn. Suddenly, the sprinkler system spouted to life, dousing Nate just as he reached Dr. Park. She was unconscious on the floor. The flames that had been licking out toward her jacket were extinguished by the sprinkler system. He pulled her toward the door as a ceiling tile fell, dropping burning embers on top of them.

Coughing hard, Nate dragged Dr. Park by her arms out the door and down the hallway through a downpour of water from the sprinkler system. An ember on her jacket hadn't been extinguished, so he slapped it out with his hand. Realizing his own jacket was smoldering, Nate shrugged the jacket off and threw it away from him. He reached the stairwell door next to the elevators and stopped. The shrill sound of the alarm was still ringing in his ears. Nate checked Dr. Park's neck for a pulse and, to his relief, found it beating strongly. She was breathing, too, but blood was trickling down her neck from an injury somewhere on her head. The air in the hall was smoky despite their distance from the source. Nate pulled open the stairway door and dragged Dr. Park onto the landing, closing the door behind him.

The air was clearer here. Nate could hear feet tromping on the stairs and voices shouting, but he couldn't make out their words over the ringing alarm.

"Is someone there? Help me!" he called out.

From below, a firefighter in full gear emerged, trotting up the stairs. Three more followed. Two large firemen stopped to assist Nate and Dr. Park while the other two continued out the door into the smoky third-floor hallway.

One firefighter put his oxygen mask over Dr. Park's face and picked her up. Nate followed the firefighter who was carrying Dr. Park down the stairs to the lobby, while the second firefighter followed Nate down the stairs.

In the lobby, they were met by paramedics, who quickly began assessing Dr. Park and shoved an oxygen mask over Nate's nose and mouth. Nate could see red blistering on Dr. Park's left hand, the one that had been closest to the burning desk. Her left jacket sleeve was scorched in places, toasted by the flames. Her face was smudged with soot, and her long, silky, brown hair was soaked and falling out of the bun she'd pinned it in. As the thought that she was remaining too still crossed his mind, Dr. Park's body was wracked by a cough, and she twisted to one side, coughing and pushing at the mask over her face.

The paramedic spoke quickly to reassure her and moved her hands away from the mask. Dr. Park's eyes flickered open in confusion before focusing on the people around her.

Nate moved closer to her side, took off his own mask, and smiled down into her green eyes.

"Hi," he said. "I'm glad I wasn't late for our appointment."

"What happened?" she asked.

"I don't know. As I stepped off the elevator on the third floor, the alarm went off. The hall smelled of smoke. I found you on the floor of your office, unconscious, with the desk on fire and the flames spreading up the wall."

"You got me out?"

"Yes."

She smiled weakly up at Nate. "Thanks," she said, coughing out the word. "Thanks for saving me."

Nate took her right hand and squeezed it, noting the firm elastic bandage cross-hatching her wrist and palm, protecting the sprain she'd sustained falling down the stairs a day earlier. A moment later, he moved back to allow the paramedics to load Dr. Park onto a gurney and wheel her away to a waiting ambulance. Given that they were already in a hospital complex, the ambulance had only to cross two parking lots to reach the emergency room. Nate refused an ambulance ride, sitting in the lobby for a few moments before a paramedic insisted on walking him the one hundred yards to the emergency room.

Four hours later, Nate sat in the police station again, this time signing a witness statement. He'd endured another questioning by the annoyed Detective Janwari, whose supervising officer was finally starting to suspect that the attacks might be connected. Fortunately, security camera time stamps from the elevator at the hospital proved that the alarm had gone off just as he had arrived on the third floor. The police knew he hadn't started the fire. Nate told the detective what he knew about the attacks on Dr. Park and Dr. King from the previous day. However, since he hadn't been present for the incidents, the police didn't want a statement from him on anything but the fire. At least, given what had happened, Nate felt he could take Dr. Park off the list of suspects. It defied logic to think that she'd killed Ingall for some unknown reason while someone else was also running around damaging the labs, hampering research, and trying to kill both Dr. Park and Dr. King.

Upon asking about Landon Piccone's whereabouts for the time of the fire, Nate was assured by the sour-voiced Janwari that the Piccones couldn't have been involved in the fire. Landon Piccone and his wife had been meeting with their daughter and a lawyer at a juvenile detention facility when the fire had broken out.

Nate thought their timing convenient and wondered whether all of Mr. Piccone's and Jeanette's followers were similarly alibied.

As he left the police station, Nate remembered that he had never gotten a chance to ask Dr. Park or Dr. King about any lab assistants or other workers at the hospital that Ingall might have known. He'd have to try again another day. Dr. Park would be kept in the hospital for observation overnight. Nate decided to let her rest and recover.

Back in his hotel room, Nate pushed his soot-covered, slightly scorched, smoke-filled clothing into a plastic laundry bag and pulled the drawstring closed before tossing it down on the floor in the closet. He'd have to get the clothes washed, buy more, or go home to San Marcos. The three sets of clothes he'd been alternately wearing since he had arrived in Houston were filthy, and he'd lost his jacket in the fire at the hospital. He'd bought a black suit for the funeral. He hadn't realized when he had left home that he would be gone so long.

The idea of going home to San Marcos seemed like a dream of an alternate reality that had nothing to do with the life he was living in Houston. Walking into his comfortable home with its shelves of academic books and journals would feel like walking into someone else's life. All the same, Nate knew he'd eventually have to go home. But not yet. Home would still be there whenever he got around to going back to it. In the meantime, he could buy some more clothes. Nate went out and made a few purchases.

Two hours later, as he was dumping his bags onto the hotel bed, Nate's phone rang.

"Hello?"

"Mr. Bryan, this is Ivan Tolokonsky. I heard about the fire at the hospital this morning. Are you okay?"

"I'm fine. I inhaled a little smoke, but not enough for the doctors to keep me at the hospital."

"I spoke to Dr. Park. She said she had smoke inhalation and minor burns. She said you saved her."

Nate ignored Tolokonsky's last sentence. "Dr. Park had some blisters on her left hand. She'll probably have both hands in bandages now, since she sprained the right one yesterday and had it wrapped already."

"I found Tullis Johnson," said Tolokonsky, a note of triumph in his voice.

"The missing employee from the camp! Do you think he leaked the story about Ingall to the media? Could he have been helping Landon Piccone's daughter organize the attack?"

"He was paid to invent and disseminate a story on Ingall. He admits that. He also admits drawing floor plans of the camp. He was paid for those, as well. He claims he didn't know the plans might be used to attack the camp. Bullshit! He knew not to come to work that night. He won't be working at the camp anymore."

"Did you give his name to the police as someone who conspired in the attack?" Nate hoped the man was still alive. He wondered what sort of methods Tolokonsky had used to get the man to admit his guilt.

"I've given his name to the police. Johnson will cooperate with them. He's been given the impression that he'll be safer in prison than in my hands." A ruthless rumbling sound came across the phone—Tolokonsky's humorless laugh.

"Is there any chance he could have killed Ingall?"

"No, he was working that night and has witnesses to confirm it. If he had anything to do with Father Ingall's murder, he would have admitted it. He is a coward. It took very little to entice him to tell me everything he knew."

Nate again pondered Tolokonsky's methods, but decided not to ask.

"Well, that resolves the leak at the camp, but not at the hospital. Whoever is responsible for the problems at the hospital may have been working for Senator Coalember. My former fiancée is on the senator's staff. I know you caught the senator accepting money from a construction company to propose laws that would isolate the children outside the city."

Tolokonsky took the revelation in stride. "Senator Coalember's hands were dirty in more ways than one. His murder this week is probably unrelated to matters here."

"I'm not so sure."

"You're not suggesting that I had him killed?" said Tolokonsky, a frigid note creeping into his voice.

"No, no," said Nate. "I don't think you killed him. However, I know the senator had a contact at the hospital. My former fiancée, Loriana, found out that the senator was paying someone to feed him information and, more importantly, to slow down the research. Maybe that person was working for both Piccone and the senator. If Ingall knew the traitor, he might have noticed something out of the ordinary in that person's behavior. Ingall was very attuned to people. If Ingall had confronted this person, whoever it is may have killed Ingall to silence him. If Ingall's murder had not been on orders from the senator, the senator might have been upset, not wanting to be linked to that murder. If the murderer realized the senator knew he'd done it and wouldn't cover for him, the murderer might have killed the senator as well."

Tolokonsky was silent for a moment. "It's possible. However, that would mean only one person leaked information to the senator, vandalized the offices, attacked the doctors, and killed Ingall and the senator to hide his guilt."

"Is it more likely that we have several people doing all of this?" Nate asked.

"Well, I can see that the incidents at the hospital are connected and that they could be connected to Father Ingall's murder, but the senator's death, too? Somehow that seems a stretch. The senator could have had any number of jealous husbands after him. Maybe he told Limestone Wells Construction's owners that he wouldn't propose the law to move the children, and they killed him."

"Maybe he was killed before he could propose the law, and that's why the senator from Louisiana made the proposal instead," said Nate.

"The senator from Louisiana is going to regret ever opening his mouth. I've sent the donation history from the construction company to the press anonymously. By tomorrow, the world will know that Senator Gilbert was paid to propose that law." Nate heard Tolokonsky's humorless, vindictive laugh again.

"Senator Gilbert is already under investigation by federal agents. Loriana told the agents everything she discovered about the bribery."

"Good," said Tolokonsky.

"Don't be surprised if agents show up at your door with questions," said Nate.

"My lawyers and I can handle their questions." Tolokonsky sounded indifferent, almost uninterested in the idea of federal agents coming to question him.

Nate bit his tongue. He wanted to make sure Tolokonsky was aware of the seriousness of the situation, but felt his words might be met with derision. "Well, I'm sure you've got the matter well in hand. I'm going to pursue the hospital leak source and whoever is hampering research." Changing the subject, Nate then added, "How is your daughter, Elizaveta?"

"Not as well as we'd hoped. She hasn't awakened as the doctors had expected."

Nate was stunned. "I'm so sorry to hear that. What do the doctors say?"

"They hope she will regain consciousness in the next few days."

"I'll say a prayer for her."

"Thank you."

Nate ended the call. Something Tolokonsky had said during the conversation had given him a flash of an idea, but it had vanished from his brain. He reviewed their discussion in his mind, but the idea, whatever it was, wouldn't return.

∾

Saturday, 3 p.m., Presbyterian Hospital.

KARIM YASSINE WAS sitting in his parents' car in the hospital parking lot with the engine running. He'd tried talking to Elizaveta, but she hadn't responded. She looked like Sleeping Beauty, touched by a poisonous spell and condemned to sleep for eternity.

Opening his backpack, he eyed his purchased supplies inside a grocery bag. He'd used the library at the school to research Piccone and his family and had confirmed what his memory had told him: He knew where they lived. If he left now, he could get there in about forty-five minutes. He'd probably be home late for dinner. Mom would be mad. He'd tell her that he had lost track of time sitting at the hospital with Elizaveta.

A tear came to the corner of his eye, and he swiped it away. He wanted to hit something, so he slammed his hands down on the steering wheel and yelled. Omar would be angry. Omar was too controlled and logical. Omar didn't understand. People like Piccone were the reason Omar couldn't live his life. People like Piccone were the real plague. Piccone deserved what he got.

Karim threw the car into gear and drove out of the parking lot toward the freeway. A quick hop on I-10 to the 610 loop north, exit Highway 290, and he was almost there. Zig-zagging through neighborhoods, Karim almost got lost. He sighed in relief when he backtracked and found the street he was looking for. Too many people were out and about. A woman was walking two Boston terriers up the tree-lined block. High-school kids were flooding off a bus, spreading out and walking off in groups of two and three. Karim parked at the end of the block and pretended to be on his phone until everyone disappeared into houses. He tugged a baseball cap down low over his face and grabbed the grocery bag. From inside the bag, he pulled out a plastic bottle, which he opened and spilled on a newly purchased kitchen washcloth. He closed the bottle and dropped it on the floorboard. Carefully, he got out of the car and strolled up the street toward the Piccone house, with the damp washcloth balled up in his hand.

As he walked, Karim scanned the area for security cameras. He spotted three covering various angles around the Piccone house. He kept his head down, looking at his feet as he moved into camera range. So far, so good.

His knees began to feel a little shaky as he turned up the walkway leading to the Piccones' front door. His stomach tightened and his breath sped up. Karim felt like is if he were running a marathon, not walking up to a house. He began to sweat profusely, large drops streaking down his back and stopping at his jeans. He focused on keeping his head down so his face couldn't be seen by any cameras.

The single step up to the porch area almost tripped him as he misjudged its height. He caught himself and barely avoided landing on his knees in front of the door. With trembling fingers he rubbed down the door knob, almost as if he were giving it a good polish. Panic rising in his throat, Karim shoved the cloth into his pocket and bolted away from the house, sprinting across the grass yard, down the block and back to his car.

He sat in the driver's seat shaking before turning the key in the ignition and executing a bad U-turn to avoid having to drive in front of the Piccone house. He'd done it, but instead of feeling excited, he felt sick. Four blocks away, he had to stop the car hastily, open the door, and vomit on the street. Frequently spitting the burning taste of stomach acid from his mouth out the window, Karim drove blindly back, but not home.

An hour later, he found himself pulling into the parking lot of the camp. He needed to see Omar. The evening visiting hours hadn't started, but the schedule was flexible on Saturdays. He would say he'd come for dinner with Omar. He'd say it was urgent.

The receptionist recognized Karim and buzzed him into the building. Noting his darting eyes and pale cheeks, she didn't question his statement that he needed to see Omar immediately. Her eyes followed the gangly, half-grown boy as he disappeared through the doors leading to the living areas. She hoped that whatever was wrong wasn't too serious. Perhaps he was worrying about Elizaveta Tolokonsky. She'd noticed that Elizaveta would sometimes linger in the lobby, waiting for a word with him.

The hollow look in Karim's eyes and the panic in his voice scared Omar. He abandoned his studies and tried not to sprint with Karim out of the room. Looking around the library, Omar could see the questions in Sandr's and Sam's eyes. He shook his head at them, letting them know that they weren't needed, and hurried his younger brother out of the room.

"We can talk in my dorm room," he said as they exited the silent library. Omar walked the now-shaking Karim down the hall and shoved him into the dorm. Omar shared the room with Sandr and Sam. The room had three beds with built-in drawers pushed against three walls. The fourth wall held closet space and a large mirror.

Karim sank down on one of the beds. His knees were Jell-O.

"What happened? What's wrong? Is it Elizaveta?"

"No. She's the same as she was. At least, I think she is. I don't know. That's not it." Karim focused on the floor, trying to summon up the anger and logic he'd conjured earlier in the day.

"Spill it!" said Omar. "You're scaring me."

"I'm killing Landon Piccone's family. They may already be dead. I don't know. I set a trap for them."

Omar dropped down in front of his brother, forcing Karim to look him in the eyes. "How? What did you do?"

"The other night when I was here, I wiped down the table with a cloth napkin. Rubbed it all over the room, really. I was going to use that, but then I realize they could trace that back to you, so I thought of something better."

Omar waited, his heart beginning to pound, but he didn't want to interrupt. He needed the whole story.

Karim looked at his brother. He could see surprise on his face, but nothing else, so he went on. "I remembered how Piccone sued the school district to keep peanuts out of his daughter's school, because she has that severe allergy. I went and read the old articles about it. Piccone said even a molecule of peanut oil left on someone's hand after eating was enough to kill his daughter if she got touched. He said she got the allergy from her mother. So I bought peanut oil and a cloth, I drove to Piccone's house, and I rubbed a washcloth full of peanut oil all over his front door knob."

"When did you do this?"

"An hour ago. I drove straight here from there."

"I see." Omar stood up and paced the room. He might already be too late to stop anyone from touching the door. Piccone would have security cameras around his house. A neighbor might identify Karim's car. The police would trace the attack back to Karim, and it would hurt them all. Besides that, it was wrong. He stopped pacing and looked at his brother. "We can't do this. We have to let someone know that the door is contaminated."

Karim jumped up from the bed, suddenly angry again. Blood pounded in his ears. "What? Why? I did it! The bastard's wife will die! Or maybe his bitch of a daughter! They deserve it for what they did to you and Elizaveta!"

"And what if they can trace the purchases back to you? What if a neighbor saw your car? What if he has security cameras?"

"I made sure I didn't show my face on camera!"

"Are you sure he doesn't have hidden cameras? Are you sure your car wasn't seen? Not to mention, what would Father Ingall say? This is wrong!"

Karim sank back down on the bed, his anger subsiding. "They almost killed Elizaveta!" He gave his brother a pleading look as tears filled his eyes. "I was so mad. It isn't fair!"

"We can't behave like terrorists and killers. The police will figure out it was you. The media will get hold of it, and people will have another reason to fear us. Right now, we need all the positive media we can get. We need the public to volunteer to help us. We'll lose support if we go around killing our enemies like crazed vigilantes." Omar was angry but trying to sound calm and reasonable. He understood his brother. He knew Karim hadn't considered all of the possible consequences, like going to jail for life, or the political ramifications of an intentional murder being linked to the children. Karim was too impulsive, too thoughtless, too immature.

"What do we do? I can't tell Mom. She'd kill me," said Karim.

"Maybe it isn't too late to undo it. The question is how to let someone know quickly without implicating you. I'd rather not see you sent to prison for attempted murder," said Omar.

The door opened and Sandr peeked in, his eyebrows up in question.

Omar waved him into the room.

"What's up?" said Sandr.

Omar gave a hasty description of what Karim had done, with Sandr listening in horror.

"Crap! Karim, have you got shit for brains?" yelled Sandr.

"Shut up, Sandr. I'm thinking. We need to get someone to that house as soon as possible," said Omar.

"Who can we send? Dr. Archepane? Ms. Jemington? If either of them go, this whole thing comes back to roost on us," said Sandr.

"If we don't get someone out there, it will come back to us no matter what. We need to get that door cleaned, preferably before the police get there." Omar ran one hand through his thick black hair and closed his eyes in thought.

"Dammit!" said Sandr, pacing the small room furiously.

"What about Father Ingall's brother?" said Omar, his eyes popping open as the thought hit him.

"That would still come back to us."

"Not if he cleans the door and pretends to be there to talk to Piccone."

"No way that'll work!" said Sandr.

"You got a better suggestion?" asked Omar, desperation in his usually calm eyes.

"No."

"Okay then. Come on!" Omar bolted out of the room and ran to find Dr. Archepane.

Luckily, the doctor was in the lounge, the first room Omar checked.

"Doctor, we need Father Ingall's brother's phone number. Right now! I'll explain later," said Omar.

CHAPTER 11

Saturday, 5 p.m.

Nate tucked his phone into his jacket pocket and raced from his hotel room to his car, praying under his breath that he wouldn't be too late.

Thirty minutes later, after a frantic stop at a superstore for supplies, he turned the car slowly down a residential street and parked unknowingly within a few feet of where Karim had parked earlier in the day.

No police cars swarmed the block. No ambulances were in view. So far, so good.

He reached into the back of his car, pulled a pair of soft knit gloves over a pair of latex gloves from his bag of new purchases, and carefully soaked them with bleach. The gloves would look odd in the warm weather, but they were the most unobtrusive method he could think of for wiping down the door knob.

Getting out of the car, he walked quickly and purposefully toward the Piccone house, surveying it as he went. The lights inside were off. Security cameras were aimed at the drive, front walk, front door, and yard. No car was parked in the drive or in front of the house. Maybe the Piccones' car was in the garage. Perhaps, like many people, they seldom used the front door to enter the house, using a garage entrance instead.

Arriving at the door, Nate glanced around the neighborhood behind him. No passersby were out jogging or walking their dogs. Hoping no neighborhood busybody was watching through blinds, Nate hurriedly and thoroughly wiped the knob, squeezing the gloves to drip bleach into all the crevices around the handle. Bleach dripped down the door under the knob. Nate wiped at it, trying to prevent it from pooling in the door frame.

Finished with his task, Nate stripped the gloves off, inverting the wet woven pair and any contaminated material that remained inside of the latex pair. He tucked the first into the second and shoved them into his pocket. He hoped the bleach didn't seep out and drip down his slacks.

The entire porch area reeked of bleach. He wondered how much of the caustic substance he'd dripped on his clothing.

Though he didn't want to do it, Nate had to knock on the door next; otherwise, his presence there would be odd if anyone reviewed the security tapes. With any luck, Piccone would be his suspicious, angry self and would refuse to shake hands or invite Nate into the house. Nate knew the bleach smell would be overwhelming inside an enclosed space. He'd have no way to explain it.

After looking the porch area and his clothes over for telltale signs of bleach, Nate knocked on the door. Then he stepped back a couple of paces. The chemical smell was nauseating.

Nate heard movement beyond the door. A dog barked and was silenced. The door swung open, revealing the exhausted face of a middle-aged woman prematurely wrinkled around the eyes. Her face looked as if the only expressions she ever used were sorrowful.

"Mrs. Piccone? Hi, I'm Nate Bryan."

"I'm not speaking to reporters," she said, and began to close the door.

"Wait, Ma'am. I'm not a reporter. My brother was Father Ingall Bryan. I'm trying to solve his murder. I know you have enough legal troubles of your own right now. You wouldn't want more heaped on you. If you could avoid more trouble, I'm sure you would."

She stopped and stared at him with skeptical eyes. "How could talking to you help me avoid legal trouble? I can't tell you anything. I don't know who killed your brother." She started to close the door again, her nose wrinkling as she noted the sharp smell of bleach.

"Wait, Ma'am. I think one of your husband's information sources at the research hospital may have killed my brother and tried to kill one of the research doctors this morning by starting a fire. The relationship, phone calls, texts, other contact between the killer and your husband will be tracked. It would be in your best interest to turn over that person's name to the police. You would avoid the appearance of having conspired to kill my brother or of having protected the identity of a killer."

"We aren't protecting any killer. What is that smell? Some kind of cleaning product?" she said, her hand coming up to her nose.

"I think one of your neighbors must be doing some heavy cleaning," said Nate with careful indifference. "Please, Ma'am. You've got legal problems enough with your daughter; having your husband linked to a murder will only compound things."

She gave Nate a bleak, joyless smile, "We won't be linked to anything. Our only informant in the research hospital had to seek other employment two months ago after being caught in a restricted area. Lots of people share our stance against those monsters. Whoever killed your brother and started that fire has no connection to us. Now go away! I have nothing else to say to you." She closed the door firmly.

Nate stared at the closed door for a few seconds, listening for movement beyond it. Then, he stepped back and hurried back to his car.

Nate drove to the nearest gas station and tossed the gloves into a dumpster next to it. He went inside to wash his hands thoroughly. His wrists were red and irritated from exposure to the bleach. Nate bought a small, overpriced tube of moisturizer in the gas station and rubbed an extra-large blob of the lotion into his skin. He opened all the windows to his car to air out the bleach smell, and then dialed Dr. Archepane at Camp Lambda.

"It's done. Tell Omar I've resolved the problem. No one got hurt." Nate promised to come to the camp soon and tell them what happened. For now, he wanted to go back to his hotel and think. If Piccone's people weren't behind the recent vandalism and attacks at the research hospital, who could it be? Someone angry at the children but not formally affiliated with the People's Health and Safety League? Someone who worked for the construction conglomerate that paid the senators? Someone working directly for Senator Coalember? Someone who fell into all three categories? Nate forced his attention back to his driving. Maybe it would be as he had told Loriana: When they found who had done it, then they'd know why.

∽

OMAR, SANDR, AND Karim left Dr. Archepane to join the others in the lounge. Family visiting time had already started. People would be waiting for them, wondering where they were.

Omar and Sandr walked side by side behind Karim, staring at his back. Sandr still wanted to bloody Karim's nose for the damage he'd almost done to them.

Omar was relieved, but still worried. Karim was too volatile. Omar couldn't leave the building to keep an eye on him like a good elder brother should. Omar couldn't say who Karim's friends were other than Elizaveta. Perhaps he had fallen in with the extremists, those who advocated the most radical tactics and devalued the lives of those without the mutation. Omar had thought Karim could see the flaw in that thinking, but now he wasn't sure. He wanted to confide in their father. Unfortunately, their father was away, working a drill site. If he were to tell their mother, she would probably agree that Karim needed better supervision, but what would she do? She might decide to send him to her parents in Saudi Arabia. That would be disastrous. Karim would rebel. He would break every rule he could. Laws were stricter over there. His punishment could be unthinkable.

Arriving at the lounge door, Karim entered first and came face to face with Ivan Tolokonsky.

"Ah, there you are," the man said, spotting his son behind Karim. "I was coming to look for you." His eyes fell on Karim's face: exhausted, beaten, and haunted, like a soldier returned from a battle in which he had not acquitted himself well. "Is something wrong?"

"Not anymore," said Omar. "How is Elizaveta?" He considered telling Mr. Tolokonsky what had happened, but wasn't sure that it was the right decision. He felt Sandr's eyes on him and hoped Sandr would stay quiet for the moment. He couldn't prevent Sandr from confiding in his father; after all, that's what he himself wanted to do with his own father. All the same, Karim wasn't ready to face whatever response might come. Omar wanted to protect Karim.

"That's what I was coming to tell you. She woke up about forty-five minutes ago. She's talking and hungry. Vera says she seems quite herself. She was asking about you, Karim. She wanted to know if you were okay. She wants to see you." Ivan studied the teenagers. He felt tension from the three boys, but was unsure of the source.

Happiness flared across Karim's face for a brief second, before it subsided suddenly. "That's wonderful," he said in a cracking voice, as if threatened by tears.

Ivan gave Karim a confused look before his son distracted him.

"That's great!" said Sandr, hugging his father.

Omar smiled and said, "That's fabulous, Mr. Tolokonsky. We're all relieved that she's okay."

Ivan looked at the three teenagers before him again. "Are you sure you're okay? Has something happened?"

Sandr saw fear fill Karim's eyes and said, "Not now. Later. It can wait."

Omar said, "Yes, later. Right now, Karim should get to the hospital to see Elizaveta before visiting hours end there. If you go straight to decon, you can make it. Hurry!" He pushed Karim toward the exit.

"Thanks," said Karim. He looked vaguely like a death-row inmate given a temporary reprieve. He turned and almost sprinted out of the room.

"What was that all about?" asked Ivan.

"It's a long story," said Omar, taking a deep breath and preparing to tell it.

❧

Sunday, 11 a.m., hotel.

THE NEXT MORNING, Nate answered his phone for a welcome break. After he had gone to church, at the invitation of Deacon Matthias, he'd planned on spending the morning researching

Limestone Wells Construction and Senator Coalember. However, all the company information he could find on the Internet only filled half a page of notes. He couldn't discover who owned it. None of the board members listed as running the company had links that he could find to the People's Health and Safety League. Searches of each individual name found little but civic events they'd attended and charities on whose boards they also sat. On the senator, he ran into an excess of information. Hundreds of news articles mentioned him, but none of the articles was likely to have anything useful in solving Ingall's murder. Nate was slowly skimming article after article when his phone rang.

"Mr. Bryan? This is Ivan Tolokonsky. I wanted to thank you for what you did yesterday. I spoke to my son and Omar last night. Karim owes you his life, and I owe you a great deal for having prevented a public-relations nightmare."

Nate noticed that preventing deaths hadn't ranked a mention except in that it had avoided negative publicity. "I'm glad no one died."

"Yes," said Ivan. "Are you absolutely certain that you neutralized the problem?"

"I thoroughly bleached the area in question. I didn't miss anything."

Ivan grunted his grudging satisfaction. Nate wondered if he'd sent someone to see to the matter as well, not trusting a job he hadn't overseen himself.

"Did you see Landon Piccone?" asked Ivan.

"No, but I spoke to his wife. Oddly enough, she did end up giving me a useful piece of information."

"Really? What was that?"

"When I said that she might have enough legal problems on her hands that she didn't need to add protecting a murderer to the list, she said that her husband's informant at the hospital had been fired two months ago and that she and her husband had nothing to do with the recent attacks. If she was telling the truth, none of the recent incidents go back to their people."

"She was probably lying," said Ivan.

"Possibly. Maybe the company that was bribing the senator has a man in the research hospital, too. I've been trying to research Limestone Wells Construction and the senator, but so far I'm getting nowhere."

"Don't bother with Limestone Wells. I know all there is to know about that company. If they had a man in the hospital, I would know it." His tone brooked no disagreement or questions.

"Okay," said Nate, deciding not to argue with Tolokonsky. He could review the matter himself later if nothing else turned up.

"Do you think you are any closer to finding your brother's killer?" asked Tolokonsky.

"If eliminating options counts as moving closer, then I'm moving closer. If all else fails, I'm going to ask Loriana to walk through the labs with me. She overheard someone speaking to the senator about slowing the research. She isn't sure, but she thinks she may be able to recognize the man's voice again."

"Tell her to be careful. If the person who killed Father Ingall is the senator's informant, her life may be in danger. Tell no one that she heard that voice."

"I already told Dr. King and Dr. Park. One of the lab assistants might have overheard as well."

"Then the secret is out! People do not know how to mind their tongues. You must assume her life is in danger." Anger and a patronizing condescension filled Tolokonsky's voice.

"I'll warn her to be careful. Right now. Goodbye," Nate said quickly.

Nate ended the call and dialed Loriana. She didn't answer. He left a message warning her to be careful, and then threw the phone down on the bed in the hotel room. Hopefully, she would be safe at the senator's offices in Austin. With federal agents everywhere around her, investigating the senator's death, no one would be able to get close enough to harm her. Maybe the killer would be stuck working in Houston and wouldn't be able to get to Austin before he could warn her of the danger. Still, he couldn't assume she was safe. He'd keep trying to call her.

Nate stared at his laptop, wishing he had the resources to check financial records. Whoever was working for the senator was being paid. Surely that money was traceable. Surely those payments would stand out in someone's bank records. He sank back down in front of the screen in thought. He tried narrowing his search parameters. Maybe the senator had links to the hospital. He typed in Memorial Hermann Research Center Hospital and Senator Coalember and watched the results appear.

Scanning the list, he found a news article about the senator visiting the research hospital on a fact-finding trip about the children. The article was ten years old. Nate clicked the link and found he'd have to pay for access to the newspaper archives. Wondering whether he was wasting his time and money, he paid the fee anyway.

The article came up. The accompanying photo showed the senator shaking hands with a former Mayor of Houston. In the background of the photo stood an array of medical personnel. Searching the faces, Nate found a younger version of Dr. King, which he had expected, but not Dr. Park. He didn't know how long she had worked at the research hospital. Nate didn't recognize any other faces, but at least half of them were obscured by people standing in front of them or by the angle from which the photo had been taken. Nate saved a copy of the photo. It didn't prove anything, but it was a tangible connection between the senator and the hospital. The article attached to the photo was biased against the children, covering the failures to treat them and the threat they might present to society in copious detail.

Nate spent the next two hours poring over articles, looking for links and finding none. His frustration increased as his attempts to contact Loriana went straight to voice mail. His concern for her safety was increasing with each passing hour. Why wouldn't she answer her phone?

Finally, a text arrived from Loriana, and Nate sighed with relief. "Got your message. Watching my back. Might have found something. Coming to Houston now."

Nate tried to call her back, but she didn't answer. Maybe she was already driving and out of cell range. He'd have to wait until she arrived to hear what she had found. Feeling on edge and jumpy, Nate decided to call Dr. Park. He'd gotten her direct number after the fire and didn't have to go through the hospital switchboard. He wondered if she was still home recovering from her injuries. He dialed and heard her solid, practical voice answer.

"Michaela Park."

"Hi, Dr. Park, this is Nate Bryan. How are you?"

"Nate, please call me Michaela."

"Fine, Michaela. How's your hand?"

"The one I burned is painful, red, and peeling a bit, but no permanent damage. The one I sprained is sore, but improving."

"You've had a rough week. Are you home or at work?"

"I'm at work. I don't like to sit at home when I have so much to do. My office is a wreck. I'm trying to see if anything is salvageable."

"Have you got a minute to talk? I had a few questions."

"Fire away," she said.

"Do you know if Ingall talked to any of the people in your lab or Dr. King's lab more than the others? Do you know if he spent a lot of time talking to anyone there in the days before he died?"

"Father Ingall had a kind word for everyone. I'm pretty sure he knew everyone's name, at the very least. He was the kind of person who could get people to open up and talk about themselves."

"True. He was well suited for being both a psychologist and a priest."

"Very," she said with a smile in her voice. She paused. "Honestly, he spent a lot of time with Dr. King and me going over details of the research, the history of the research especially. Father Ingall liked to know the background of everything. He had reconstructed how one project led to another, and one study built on a previous one to see how we'd arrived where we are today. Father Ingall probably had a better working knowledge of the various projects at the hospital, both successful and unsuccessful, than anyone, other than Dr. King, who has been here the longest and has overseen the majority of the work."

Recalling her absence from the ten-year-old article he'd found, Nate asked, "When did you start working there?"

"Nine years ago. I'd read everything Dr. King had published, and this was my dream job. It still is."

"You always wanted to go into research about the children, then?" asked Nate out of curiosity.

"Yes. The first cases appeared when I was twelve. Every news article I saw fascinated me. My parents were both doctors researching rare genetic diseases. I heard them talking about the need for research to help the children with the double mutations. They were always sympathetic with the children. Working here was my life's goal. I wanted to make a difference for the children."

"And you did it." An idea occurred to Nate. If Ingall had been looking into the past, maybe he should, too. Maybe the slowing of the research wasn't a new event. Maybe it had been going on for years, and Ingall had noticed a pattern. "Tell me, what was the state of the research when you arrived to work there nine years ago?"

"Dr. King and his team had managed to work out the location of the gene mutation and had spent years tracing how it caused the toxin to be created and secreted. They'd worked out the chemical composition of the toxin and how it worked against noncarriers of the mutation. One section of the lab spent years trying to trace the origins of the mutation by studying the families that had it. They worked out the connection between the petroleum industry and the antihistamine, finding those two factors in every single family. However, as I told you before, we will probably never be able to prove the cause. At the same time, lots of people were trying to come up with treatments and cures, but getting nowhere."

"What made you decide to look at treating the rest of the population instead of trying to cure the children?"

"Well, when I looked at the research, I wanted to look at things from an angle that hadn't been tried. I asked myself whether the mutation had any positive effects for the carriers. No one had done any studies or documented the health effects of the mutation on the carriers. So I started with a general overview of the health of the children and their parents. That's when I found not a single case of cancer in any of them. That stood out like a huge red flag. Thousands of people and not one single case of cancer. The odds of that happening were astronomical. So I started looking at other things from the common to the uncommon, asthma and allergies to lupus and juvenile rheumatoid arthritis. I found the usual viral infections, but with a quicker recovery period. I found eye diseases and tooth decay. I found heart problems. When I put together the list of things they didn't suffer from, I realized many of the conditions they lacked were immunological. That's when it hit me that the mutation might have positive effects for the population and might help treat immunological pathologies."

"Sounds logical to me. How did everyone else take the idea, initially?" asked Nate. The dormant researcher in him was fascinated.

"At first, I faced a lot of skepticism. People thought I'd simply missed finding carriers with the various diseases. No one wanted to consider that the mutation might have a positive side. They were too busy looking for treatments."

"Did you run into opposition to your research?"

She laughed. "You could call it that. I almost lost grants three times in the last nine years. Each time, I had to fight to prove the validity of my research to keep my funding."

"Do you think that someone might have been trying to stymie you, to block your work?"

"You mean any one individual? No." She sounded certain of herself and her knowledge of her lab.

"Did Dr. King have similar funding problems?"

"No, but his work was more along the accepted lines. He wasn't going against the grain." She laughed a little.

"What new information has come out of Dr. King's lab in the last few years? Were there any studies that looked promising, and then didn't come out as expected? Anything where someone might have tampered with results to prevent a new line of study from being followed?" he asked.

"Hmm," she said, thinking. "One study puzzled me. Three years ago, a researcher in Dr. King's lab thought he'd found a way to neutralize the skin toxin. There was a lot of excited gossip, since it looked so positive. The researcher, Porter Scotland, spent two years trying to replicate his initial findings before he gave up. He was never able to replicate his findings. He quit and went to work at UT Southwestern in Dallas." She paused, and Nate waited for her to continue. "Now that I think about it, Dr. King's lab has had a lot of studies not come out well. Some were found to have flaws after the fact, such as variables that affected the outcome that the researcher had failed to account for, but others had inconsistent results."

"So the idea that someone was interfering with studies could have validity?"

"It's terrible to think, but it's possible."

"If you looked at the failed or inconsistent studies, do you think you could identify who might have been able to interfere with them?" Nate asked.

"Maybe. But with that many studies, I don't know who would have had access to them all."

"Could we look?" asked Nate. "I don't think I'll have any problems interpreting the studies. I do have something of a background in research."

She laughed out loud, not a gentle feminine laugh, but a strong, full-throated chuckle. "You'd be the perfect person to help me wade through all that research material. This saboteur in the lab needs to be found! I can't stand the idea of someone purposely destroying years of scientific work!"

"Can we start looking today? Are you free?" asked Nate.

"Absolutely. Meet me at the hospital," she said.

"On my way," said Nate.

Chapter 12

Sunday, 6 p.m., Memorial Hermann Research Center Hospital.

Nate sat and stretched in his chair. His back needed to pop somewhere in the lumbar region, and his foot was asleep. He glanced at Dr. Park, her eyes still skimming through names, occasionally shifting to the notepad next to her on which she'd been adding names to various lists. They'd been trolling through ten years' worth of research studies for the last four hours. In the first hour, they'd found several names in common with the first three years of studies, but as their search progressed, the names they'd found failed to reappear in later studies. They'd decided that perhaps the interference had begun later, maybe only in the last few years. Nate's eyes were tired. He was beginning to get frustrated, but Michaela Park was still working with the same intensity as when she had started. He smiled in admiration as he looked at her face, still totally absorbed in her work. Her fingers moved quickly on the keyboard, the only parts of her hands free from bandages.

"Michaela, I haven't found any single name in common on the questionable or failed studies. Have you?"

Her eyes popped up from her computer and met his. "No, nothing yet. How much more do you have to go?"

"I'm up to this year already. If there had been long-term sabotage, I think I'd have seen evidence of it by now."

She sat back into her chair and stretched out her legs. "I've only got this year's studies to review as well. We must have overlooked someone. Who could have had access to all the labs, to all the results? Someone whose presence would be considered normal? Could someone on a night cleaning crew have been involved?"

"Would they have had the skills to tamper with results in a way that wouldn't be noticed?" Nate asked with a doubtful look.

"If that's what they were hired to do, maybe." She leaned forward, her elbows on the desk, one hand under her chin. "I see another pattern emerging, though. It's just so crazy that it seems impossible."

"What is it?" Nate sat up straight, alert. The craziest of ideas could be the answer. After all, they had eliminated all the obvious ones.

"It's just a feeling right now. Nothing with solid proof. What I'm seeing could be honest errors."

"What is it?"

"Let me keep looking into this. I need to look a little more before I say anything. Jobs and reputations are on the line here. The people I work with deserve that we get this right."

"At least give me an idea of what you're looking at. Not to be pessimistic, but you've been attacked twice recently in ways that could have killed you. What if the next attack succeeds? Someone needs to know what you know."

Her green eyes widened slightly, and she frowned at him in dismay. "I hadn't thought about that. Fine. I'll explain."

Nate's phone rang. He glanced at it. "Hold that thought. Loriana is calling. She texted me that she'd found something, too."

"Go ahead. I need to organize my thoughts anyway," said Dr. Park, waving a hand in permission for him to answer.

"Hello? This is Nate."

"Hi, Nate. I'm arriving at the hospital. Can you meet me here?" said Loriana.

"I'm already here with Dr. Park. We had an idea about how to find who might be the senator's insider in the labs here."

"Oh, good. Meet me in the lobby in ten minutes. I want to show you something."

"What is it?" asked Nate, hoping at last he had a real lead to follow.

"When I get there. I'm in traffic. I hate Houston traffic. See you soon." The call ended.

Nate looked at Dr. Park, who was lost deep in thought, staring into blank space.

"Dr. Park? Michaela?" he prompted.

"Sorry. I'm trying to work this out in my head."

"Tell me what you see," Nate said with an encouraging grin.

Nothing concrete. I'm not even sure that what I'm seeing isn't normal," she said, with a troubled frown causing a crease between her eyebrows.

"Tell me anyway," said Nate.

"Looking at the various projects and studies done in the last ten years, a number of them had flaws from the start. Missed controls for variables, unexpected interactions that made the results skewed."

"So?" Nate didn't think that was too unusual. Sometimes things got missed.

"So, a few of them are the kinds of things that might have been caught when the study was proposed. There are no egregious errors, mind you. What I'm seeing may well be the kind of errors commonly caught upon peer review."

"Okay," he said, "go on."

"But, then again, there are a lot of them. To know if the number I'm seeing is excessive, I'd have to do this kind of review on ten or twenty or fifty other labs to see if our errors grossly exceeded anyone else's." She sat back in her chair in frustration.

"I see," he said, feeling frustrated along with her.

A troubled look filled Dr. Park's green eyes. "That kind of review would take me months to complete, provided I could get cooperation from enough other labs for it to be valid."

"Then, let's look at what we started out to do. Did you see any single person associated with any of the questionable studies?"

"No."

Nate stood up and shrugged his shoulders to stretch. "Well, then we're at another dead end. Come on. Let's go down to the lobby. Loriana should be arriving here soon. We can wait for her down there. We could use a coffee and some walking to wake up."

Dr. Park grinned, "This time I'll walk down the stairs, no need for anyone to carry me."

Nate laughed. Although they hadn't accomplished anything, he was enjoying his time with her. "You have no idea how happy that makes me."

They left the conference room in which they'd been working, since Dr. Park's office was a scorched, taped-off disaster. They walked down the stairs and made their way to the cafeteria, purchased coffees, and went to drink them in the lobby.

Fifteen minutes later, Nate strolled to a nearby trash can to throw away his empty cup. He glanced at this watch. Loriana still hadn't appeared. Perhaps she'd underestimated the time it would take her to arrive.

Dr. Park said, "Maybe she's stuck in traffic?"

"Maybe."

Suddenly a woman raced in through the sliding-glass doors and ran straight to the reception desk. She was blonde and matronly, not Loriana. Her agitated voice rose in volume as she spoke.

"Call the police. There's a body, a woman, she's dead! Murdered in the parking lot!"

Nate and Dr. Park looked at each other before they both sprinted out the glass doors. A crowd was forming around a car in the parking lot, three rows of cars away from the entrance. Nate outpaced Dr. Park and arrived first, pushing past the onlookers to get closer.

The body of a woman was sprawled on the ground between the cars. Her lips were blue tinged, and her brown, lifeless eyes were staring. A piece of medical tubing was cutting into her lovely throat. A button on her v-necked blouse had come undone, exposing a lace-covered bra over ample cleavage. One hand was grasping uselessly at the tube around her throat. Loriana Montilla was dead.

Nate felt like he'd been kicked in the gut. He stifled the urge to yank the tubing off of Loriana's throat. A doctor was kneeling next to her. He felt for a pulse and checked for breathing. He looked up at the gathering crowd and shook his head.

Gulping hard, Nate forced himself to concentrate. She'd been bringing him something. Where was her purse? Nate looked under the cars but didn't spy her purse anywhere. Her hands were empty. If she'd had something with her, something to show him, it was gone now.

Nate walked back to Dr. Park. Sirens were sounding in the distance. "This is my fault. I told you and Dr. King that Loriana thought she might be able to identify the lab saboteur by his voice. One of your employees overheard me. He could have told anyone. Hell, he may even be the one. Anyone outside the door could have heard me. When I told Ivan Tolokonsky that she might be able to identify the saboteur, he told me to make sure no one knew. He said she might be in danger. I called and left her messages to be careful, to watch her back." His voice shook and his hand trembled as he ran it through his thin red hair.

"It's not your fault. What should we do? Wait for the police?" Dr. Park put one hand gently on Nate's shoulder and rubbed his upper arm.

Rage slammed through Nate, convulsing his face into an angry mask. He fought to control himself. Every inch of him wanted to pound a car in the parking lot, kick the lights out, and dent the hood. He kept telling himself it was a pointless waste of energy, but that didn't stop him from kicking his foot into the nearest car's rear tire. "Can we find out if that red-headed employee of yours is in the building?"

"Zack?" Dr. Park stepped back from Nate, astounded and worried by his reaction.

"The one who brought you pain medicine before the press conference." Nate said the words through gritted teeth. He wanted to put his hands around someone's throat. Someone had to pay for ripping away the people closest to him.

"That was Zack, but it couldn't be him. He's only been working here for six months."

"We need to know what he heard and who he told."

"I see. What about the police? The . . . body?"

"We need to solve this before anyone else dies. The police haven't done anything. Have they even been here to talk to you about Ingall?" Nate tried to hold his voice down, tried not to yell, but the seething anger in his voice was unmistakable.

"No, they haven't. All right. Let's go find Zack."

Police cars with glowing red and blue lights were pulling into the parking lot as Nate and Dr. Park hurried back into the hospital and up the stairs. They walked through a number of labs, but as it was already past dinner time, most of the employees were gone for the day.

After passing through yet another empty room, Dr. Park said, "Let's try Dr. King's offices and labs."

They went up the stairs again to the next level and found suite 485. Dr. Park pushed the door open and called out, "Hello?"

"I'm back here. Dr. Park, is that you?" came Dr. King's voice.

Nate and Dr. Park walked past the front reception desk, down a hall of offices toward where the voice had come from.

"Yes. It's me. I was looking for Zack. Have you seen him?" They entered an office and found Dr. King seated at a desk with files of paperwork spread out before him and a stack of medical journals at his elbow.

"Zack? No, not since about five-thirty. I think he's gone for the day."

"We have bad news, Dr. King," said Nate. The anger in his voice was more controlled now that some pent-up energy had been expelled while climbing the stairs. "Loriana Montilla, the woman who worked for Senator Coalember, who'd heard the voice of the mole in the labs here, was found dead in the parking lot a few minutes ago."

A deep furrow formed between the doctor's eyes. "No! That's terrible! What happened?"

"She was strangled with a piece of tubing. Doctor, did you tell anyone, anyone at all, that she might be able to identify the person causing the trouble here?"

"Tell anyone? No!"

"Neither did I," said Dr. Park.

"The only other person who might have known was Zack," Nate said. "Are you sure he left?"

"He said he was leaving, but I didn't follow him to the parking lot to see. I suppose he could still be here. Do you think he killed her?"

"Not necessarily. But we need to know if he told anyone else that she might be able to identify our vandal and the source of our leaks here," said Dr. Park.

"Do you want me to help you look for him?" Dr. King asked.

"No, thank you," said Dr. Park. "Please lock your door. I don't want anyone to sneak up on you. We've had too many incidents here lately."

"I'll do that." Dr. King stood up behind his desk, preparing to escort them out.

Nate turned and walked down the hall to the small reception area. As he reached the desk, he glanced down at an open-mouthed, rectangular trash can. A pair of wadded-up, disposable gloves peeked out from under a balled-up piece of paper. They reminded him of the gloves he'd balled up and tossed after cleaning the Piccones' door knob. Hiding the evidence.

Suddenly, the pieces in his mind began to click into place. He stopped walking. Dr. Park, chatting with Dr. King as she walked, paused to see why he'd stopped.

Nate tried to make his face blank, but he wasn't quick enough. She saw the pale look of comprehension and hatred on his face.

"What? What is it? Did you think of something?" she asked.

Nate fought for control. He didn't want to endanger Dr. Park. She was standing between him and Dr. King. "I was thinking that we need to call Detective Janwari, but then I realized he might try to pin Loriana's death on me. I can't believe she's dead."

Dr. Park was sympathetic. "The shock must be hitting you. Do you need to sit down? Don't worry about being accused of murder. I was with you the whole time. We're probably on surveillance video in the lobby waiting for her. Even if they suspect you, you'll be cleared immediately."

"You're right. We should call the detective and get it all over with, the sooner the better. You go ahead downstairs and bring the police back up here. I want a word with Dr. King."

Nate started toward the door to usher Dr. Park out, but he looked at Dr. King in time to see the doctor glance from the trash can to Nate. The doctor rushed to block Nate's progress toward the door.

CHAPTER 13

"You aren't going anywhere. We're all staying right here." Dr. King locked the office door and crossed his arms on his chest.

"What do you mean?" asked Dr. Park, her eyes clouding as she looked from Nate to Dr. King.

Nate and Dr. King stared at each other for a long moment. Nate sized up his chances in tackling the older man.

"Don't try anything," said Dr. King, moving his hand to the small of his back under his white coat. The hand re-emerged with a pistol.

Nate eyed the gun and looked for a way to get himself and Dr. Park out of the line of fire.

"Both of you, slide your phones toward me across the floor," said Dr. King.

"It was you, Willett! Damn it!" Dr. Park said. "We reviewed all the failed or equivocal research projects from the last ten years. I couldn't find a single common factor, not a single person who was linked to each study, but you had access to all of them. Your reputation is staked to our success. I thought there was no way you would tamper with studies, no way you would allow errors to creep into studies! How could you?" Her green eyes sparked with anger. Red circles appeared on her cheeks. She didn't seem to be paying any attention to the gun.

"Easily. I'm the first to arrive in the morning and the last to leave. No one pays any attention to me wandering through the labs, checking to see that everything is running smoothly. Now give me your phone!"

"But why?" Dr. Park asked.

Nate thought she might slap Dr. King or try to claw his eyes out, if she didn't burst into flames from anger first. Somehow, her rising anger helped cool his. The fog of anger lifted, and Nate took advantage of Dr. King's momentary distraction. He held down the emergency call button on his phone as he bent to place the phone screen down on the floor. Then, he kicked it toward the doctor, aiming for it to go under the desk rather than to the doctor. Hopefully, 911 services would answer and start recording.

"Many reasons, mostly financial, others personal," said Dr. King, holding his gun steady and aimed at Dr. Park.

"Put the gun away, Dr. King. What are you going to do, shoot us? Everyone would hear the shots and come running," said Nate as loudly as he could, for the sake of the 911 operator.

"By the time they break through the door, I'll be on the floor, shot in the arm. I'll tell them that you shot Dr. Park in a fit of madness, accusing her of having killed your brother. I'll say that I wrestled with you to get the gun, and you shot me in the arm before I got the gun away, and I shot you in self-defense."

Dr. Park was still screaming mad. "I don't understand! It was your life's work, and you were sabotaging everyone who was building on the foundation you created! How could you?" She removed her phone from her pocket and threw it at Dr. King's head.

Dr. King dodged sideways with aplomb. The phone slammed into the wall behind him and crashed to the floor. "Think of it this way: Once you're dead, Dr. Park, who will run your study? Naturally, it will fall into my hands. The results will be published under my name. Who will get the credit for the breakthrough of the century? Your name will, of course, be remembered, but dead people can't collect Nobel Prizes. I will be the only one credited with all the major advances in the field. No one will surpass me. Making sure no one surpasses my achievements has been profitable in many ways."

"You burned my office and tried to kill me because you were jealous of my success? It could have been *your* success if you'd allowed studies to be properly conducted!"

"No, I don't think so. I ran out of original thoughts years ago. Completely burned out. My inspiration dried up, and I stopped caring. The only way to stay on top was to keep everyone else down or supervise other people's ideas to keep my hand in the game. All major successful studies came from under my supervision. Those that I didn't have a hand in directly were blocked. I was succeeding, with quite elegant methods, until you came along and set up your own lab. At first, I thought your ideas were too crazy to work. I didn't bother to interfere because I thought there was no way you would produce anything viable."

"Ingall recognized your jealousy, your anger, your insane arrogance and need for self-aggrandizement," Nate said. "He looked at the history of the work done here, and he put the pieces together. He realized what you had been doing, didn't he? That's why you killed him."

"He tried to talk to me. To help me see the error of my ways. He threatened to expose me. I played along, acted remorseful, and asked to meet with him privately. And he agree to it. He walked out and shook my hand, stupid fool, right before I shot him. Just like I'm going to shoot you."

"This has gone far enough. You killed Loriana, too, didn't you? You knew she might recognize your voice. How did you know she was coming here tonight?"

"I didn't, that was luck. I had planned on simply avoiding her when you brought her around. But then I saw her in the parking lot, getting out of her car when I came back in from dinner. I always come back after dinner. By then everyone is usually gone, and I have free reign in the labs."

"How did you know what she looked like?"

"Her picture is on Senator Coalember's website, along with her title. I made sure to look her up when you told me that she might be able to recognize my voice."

"So you went out and killed her?" replied Dr. Park, aghast.

"Of course, you stupid woman. She was a loose end that I couldn't afford. When opportunity appears like that, I always take advantage of it." His face lacked all warmth and all empathy. His best interest was all that mattered. Other lives were nothing in the face of his wants.

Nate wondered whether the people at 911 were still listening. He needed to give them better clues. "Dr. King, the police are already here, outside the hospital in the parking lot investigating Loriana's death. They could be up here in a matter of seconds once gunshots are heard. You can't get away with four murders. Statistically, you're done! They will catch you. The gloves you wore to kill Loriana are in the trash right there. Her DNA will be on them along with your own. You can't hide the evidence fast enough. There's no point in this. You are caught!"

"The police may be in the parking lot, but that doesn't concern me. They won't get here fast enough for you and Dr. Park. Then, respected individual that I am, I can tell them any story I want. I can put the gloves in your pocket and blame that murder on you. I can arrange things any way I wish. Besides, your count is wrong. We'll be up to five murders once I kill you two. You forgot about the senator."

Nate really hoped the police were listening and that some-one was coming soon. He didn't know how much longer he could keep the doctor talking. He considered grabbing for the gun, but knew it to be foolhardy. He'd get shot in the process. Then a voice in his head answered that concern: *So what if you get shot? While you fight for the gun, Dr. Park could escape. You could save Dr. Park.*

Nate agreed with the voice whispering in his ear. He lunged for the gun, knocking it upward as he held onto the doctor's hand, which only tightened its grip on the gun. As Nate tried to pry the weapon away, the doctor fired into the ceiling.

"Run, Michaela! Get help!" Nate yelled.

Suddenly, a heavy weight crashed into the two men as they struggled for the gun, knocking them both to the ground. Long brown hair fell in Nate's face as he rolled on the floor trying to pin down the older man.

Dr. Park rolled away from the dog pile she'd created and flung herself across Dr. King's head and shoulders.

Nate pinned the older man's torso as Dr. Park ripped the gun from his hand.

"Are you crazy? Why would I leave you to fight him by yourself?" she asked, as she stood up with Dr. King's gun in her hand.

Yelling voices came from outside the office. The door came crashing off its hinges as two policemen with guns drawn plunged into the room.

~

Wednesday, 5 p.m., Camp Lambda.

Four hours after Loriana's funeral ended, Nate and Dr. Park presented themselves at Camp Lambda for long-awaited explanations. The student lounge at Camp Lambda was packed, filled to capacity. What looked like a couple hundred curious faces craned to see Nate and Dr. Park. Nate hoped the fire marshal didn't decide to drop in for a surprise inspection. Everyone in the building deserved an explanation, and the news coverage had been woefully inadequate so far. Between the police refusing to discuss an ongoing investigation and the media's inability to put the pieces together correctly, many people had no idea of the extent of the situation until Nate and Dr. Park came to explain it to Dr. Archepane, Ms. Jemington, and Mr. and Mrs. Tolokonsky. Those four had insisted on this larger gathering, so that the families and children could hear firsthand what had happened.

"Senator Coalember visited Dr. Willett King at his lab almost ten years ago," Nate began, wondering if he should have put together a presentation that included the picture they had found of the senator and the doctor together. "We know that they met and talked about the state of the ongoing research. At that point in time, the doctor had little hope for a cure. No promising ideas were on the horizon, and things looked grim. We don't know if the senator asked him to see that it stayed that way then, or if that happened at a later point in time. However, the records suggest that, at some point, Dr. King began to interfere in the research, allowing errors to creep into studies and tampering with results, and receiving money from the senator in exchange. The police and federal law enforcement are looking for proof of the payments that the doctor received from the senator."

Nate paused to let his words sink in. Though most had heard the rumors, many hadn't wanted to believe Dr. King was involved. Even the police hadn't wanted to believe it at first. Nate thought back to the questioning he'd received from Detective Janwari, who initially had laughed at the whole story. The detective had suggested that Nate was concocting a conspiracy theory out of nothing, before two FBI agents had taken over the case. The FBI had been much more receptive to Nate's version of events. They were the ones following the money. They'd even found evidence of Dr. King's presence at the senator's home.

Nate took a breath and continued the explanation. "By his own admission, Dr. King initially ignored Dr. Park's work because he thought it had little chance of succeeding. Only in the last year or so did he start to pay attention to her, leaking information about her work to the senator and vandalizing her lab and his own, to keep suspicion off himself. About six months ago, he was overheard meeting with the senator, discussing what he was doing to prevent medical advances. Loriana Montilla, an aide to the senator, overheard that meeting and later saw proof that the senator was being paid by a company looking to profit off your situation here. The company, Limestone Wells Construction, wanted to build a prison facility out in West Texas to isolate y'all outside of populated areas. Really, they wanted to profit off your misery and pretend it was all a matter of public safety. The construction company paid several senators to get them to propose a law requiring that you all be housed outside of populated areas. The senator from Louisiana followed through and made that proposal last week."

An angry grumbling rose from the crowd.

Dr. Park stepped forward and said, "I know this is hard to hear. However, we have prevented this. That law will never pass now! Never!" She stepped back. "Sorry, Nate, please continue."

Nate smiled grimly. The whole situation still angered him. He hoped the people involved were found guilty of their crimes, particularly those looking to profit off other people's misery.

He regained his train of thought and continued. "My brother, Father Ingall Bryan, discovered that Dr. King was hampering research at the hospital. Ingall threatened to expose him if he didn't stop, so Dr. King killed Ingall. I can only speculate what happened next. We think that when the senator realized Dr. King had killed Ingall, the senator was angry and didn't want to be involved. Or, maybe, Dr. King decided it was time to stop working for the senator and get back to doing real work again after getting rid of Dr. Park, in order to take over her study. In any case, we believe Dr. King killed the senator by putting an overdose of heart medicine in his drink."

Eyes in the crowd shifted from Nate to Dr. Park. He knew they'd heard about the attacks on her.

Nate said, "Dr. King tried repeatedly to kill Dr. Park, setting traps for her and burning her office. At the same time, he pretended that he, too, had been attacked. His goal was to be in charge of Dr. Park's ongoing work so that he would remain the leading expert and researcher in the field. He wanted all the accolades for himself."

Now came the hard part, admitting that he'd put Loriana in danger, admitting that his actions had led to her death. Nate felt a wave of guilt run through him and his eyes burned. He blinked rapidly to keep his emotions in check, something he'd been struggling with all day. The funeral had been hard, but this was harder still.

"I, not knowing that Dr. King was dangerous, told him that Ms. Montilla might be able to identify the mole's voice and that she was looking for a connection between the senator and the hospital. She found a letter from Dr. King to the senator in the files. The letter was basically innocuous, but it did establish a connection between the two men. A copy of that letter was found in Dr. King's pocket the night he was arrested, shortly after he killed Ms. Montilla. He had strangled her when he happened to see her arriving at the hospital."

Nate could see sympathy in the eyes of the people in front of him. Their sympathy did nothing to assuage his guilt. He glanced at Dr. Park. She wasn't looking at him. Her eyes were focused on nothing. He could see she was lost in thought. He wondered if she, too, was haunted by the memory of Loriana's lifeless body.

"Dr. Park and I, that same day, had spent hours reviewing research studies at the hospital, looking for evidence of tampering, evidence of anyone who might have interfered with the studies. We couldn't find anyone linked to every single failed research project. It wasn't until after Ms. Montilla was killed that we knew Dr. King was responsible. He was always in the building and had access to everything. When he realized that we knew he was guilty, he pulled a gun on Dr. Park and me. He intended to kill us. Dr. Park and I were able to get the gun away from him just as the police arrived. The police collected disposable gloves from Dr. King's trash can. Ms. Montilla's DNA was on the gloves. The police also told me that ballistics for Dr. King's gun match the bullet that killed Ingall."

Detective Janwari had called to share that bit of news. Nate could still hear the anger in the detective's voice. Nate wondered if people like the detective, those most entrenched in their opinions, would ever get over their hurt and anger. Would they ever see that the children weren't to blame? Or would it take new, more open-minded generations being born and growing up before the suspicion and fear of the children died. If someone like the detective could be brought to see the reality of the situation, and could be convinced of Dr.

Park's solution, they would win the public relations battle. He'd discussed the question with Dr. Park, who took a very optimistic view. She believed that they could change the hearts and minds of the people. Nate hoped she was right.

Nate wrapped up his comments to the crowd. He'd been speaking long enough. "Dr. Park and I have no doubt as to Dr. King's guilt in all of this. The judicial system probably won't get around to trying him for months, if not a year. In the meantime, the vaccine trials will move forward under Dr. Park's supervision."

Nate stopped speaking and looked out at the stunned faces in the crowd before him. They began talking among themselves. Nate felt sure questions were coming. He spotted Omar moving toward him.

Omar stepped to the front of the crowd. "So a construction company bribed the senator, and the senator paid Dr. King to slow down research. Father Ingall found out what Dr. King was doing and confronted him, so Dr. King killed him. Then Dr. King killed the senator to . . . what, clean up loose ends? Because the senator figured out he killed Father Ingall?"

"That's what we think happened, yes," said Nate. "But we think Dr. King had been interfering with research for years, even before he was paid to do it."

Dr. Park came forward to answer Omar. "He was greedy and arrogant and wanted to keep any accolades on research about your condition to himself," she said. "Dr. King wanted to be the only expert, the leader in his field. It suited him to take money from the senator to block other people's studies, getting paid to do something he would have done anyway. His attacks on me were out of spite and jealousy, and to get me out of the way in order to usurp my work."

Ivan Tolokonsky and his family had been standing to one side, near the front. Ivan came out next to Nate and Dr. Park.

His eyes scanned the crowd, and then he spoke. "On behalf of everyone here, I'd like to thank you, Mr. Bryan, and you, Dr. Park, for your work in solving this and exposing Dr. King. We look forward to the upcoming vaccine trials." He shook hands with Nate and Dr. Park, and then he began to clap.

The room exploded into applause and cheers. The meeting broke up. People began to move around the room as best they could in the press of the crowd, congregating in smalls groups to discuss what they'd heard or coming up to shake Nate's hand and greet Dr. Park.

A shame-faced teenage boy with curly, black hair and a nose too big for his face presented himself to Nate with a glowing Elizaveta Tolokonsky by his side. "Mr. Bryan, I'm Omar's brother, Karim. I wanted to thank you for undoing the damage I almost caused. I'm sorry. I. . ." His words trailed off to silence, and he looked for forgiveness or at least understanding in Nate's face.

"Anger is a powerful emotion. I fought with my temper my whole life. More than once I got in trouble when I was your age for letting my anger control me," Nate replied kindly. "We all make mistakes. We have to learn to live with the consequences of them and not repeat them." He reached out to shake Karim's hand.

"Yes, Sir. I'm learning," said Karim, who shook his hand briefly and then retreated hastily, with Elizaveta holding his hand.

Nate glanced around to see Omar's watchful, intelligent eyes track his younger brother across the room. Nate gave Omar a nod, and Omar nodded back before walking over to Nate.

"Soon you'll be out of here," Nate said to Omar.

"The research will take time, maybe years," said Omar. "However, Mr. Tolokonsky has come up with another idea.

We are going to take a page from Landon Piccone's playbook and file a lawsuit. I'm legally an adult, and I'm being confined against my will. We're hoping to force a trial on whether my rights are being violated. The legal process could also take years, but, in the meantime, I expect to show up in courts regularly and keep our plight in the news. The more often I go to court without someone dropping dead because of me, the more unreasonable it will seem to keep me in quarantine."

"Sounds like a solid plan," said Nate.

"I'm going to drag Karim into doing legal research for me. It should keep him busy, and keep him where either I or Mr. Tolokonsky can keep an eye on him."

"He seems to have learned his lesson," Nate said. "He may not need too much watching."

Omar smiled. "I hope you're right."

Dr. Archepane and Ms. Jemington appeared from somewhere in the crowd. "Have you heard?" asked the white-maned doctor with the age spots on his face. "Landon Piccone announced today that he is stepping down from his leadership of the People's Health and Safety League. We're hoping that, without his leadership, the whole organization will implode and cease to exist."

"That would be great. Have they decided whether to charge his daughter as an adult for organizing the assault on this place?" Nate asked.

"That hearing is scheduled for next week," said Ms. Jemington. "Her parents are submitting some sort of psychological testing results on her level of brain development."

"In spite of what she did," said Dr. Archepane, "I'm not sure I want to see her charged as an adult. Her entire childhood was poisoned by her father's drive for vengeance, but I've long believed in the flexibility of youth and the value of rehabilitation. She could still be a contributing member of society, given time and therapy. Youth can truly repent and reform if given the chance."

Ms. Jemington looked skeptical, but didn't disagree. Omar looked thoughtful.

Nate hadn't given Jeanette Piccone's future much thought, but he thought Ingall would have agreed with Dr. Archepane. If Karim deserved a second chance, why didn't Jeanette?

An hour later, Nate was tired and ready to go home, but only so that he could prepare to come back frequently. The trials would begin soon. Dr. Park had assured him that he would be hearing from her regularly. He did, after all, have a Ph.D. in biochemistry. They spoke the same language. If this went on, Nate might have to get around to asking Dr. Park her views on religion. Nate could almost see Ingall smiling at that thought.

It still physically hurt to think of Ingall. Nate knew that the day-to-day pain from losing Ingall would decrease eventually, but the wound was permanent. He would learn to live without Ingall's physical presence. He hoped he would reach a time where happy memories returned and no longer hurt. Nate looked around the room, knowing Ingall's spirit was looking out for all of these people. Life would go on. The battle for the children's rights would go on. Nate had his own path to follow, until his time came to join Ingall.

About the Author

N. M. CEDEÑO lives in Texas and writes mystery short stories and novels. Her mysteries vary from traditional mysteries, to suspense, to science fiction in genre. Her romantic suspense novel, *All In Her Head*, was published in 2014 by Lucky Bat Books. Her science fiction mystery "A Reasonable Expectation of Privacy" was published by *Analog Science Fiction and Fact Magazine* in 2012, and is available online. For more information please visit nmcedeno.com.

Other Stories by N. M. Cedeño

If you enjoyed this story, you may also like:

Near Future Crime and Mystery Short Stories:
"A Reasonable Expectation of Privacy"
"In the Interest of Public Safety"
"Pariah"

Suspense / Mystery Novels:
All in Her Head

Connect with N. M. Cedeño

To connect with N. M. Cedeño please visit
nmcedeno.com